Welcome to Our Hillbrow

Welcome to Our

A NOVEL OF POSTAPARTHEID SOUTH AFRICA

HILLBROW

PHASWANE MPE

Introduction by Ghirmai Negash

OHIO UNIVERSITY PRESS
ATHENS

Ohio University Press, Athens, Ohio 45701
www.ohioswallow.com
© 2011 by Ohio University Press
All rights reserved

First published by University of Natal Press
Private Bag X01, Scottsville, 3209, South Africa
E-mail: books@nu.ac.za
© Phaswane Mpe 2000
First published in 2001

Printed in the United States of America
Ohio University Press books are printed on acid-free paper ⊚ ™

20 19 18 17 16 15 14 13 12 11   5 4 3 2 1

Library of Congress Cataloging-in-Publication Data
Mpe, Phaswane, 1970–2004.
 Welcome to our Hillbrow : a novel of postapartheid South Africa /
Phaswane Mpe ; introduction by Ghirmai Negash.
    p. cm.
 "First published by University of Natal Press ... Scottsville, South Africa,
2001"—T.p. verso.
 Summary: "Welcome to Our Hillbrow is an exhilarating and disturbing ride
through the chaotic and hyper-real zone of Hillbrow—microcosm of all that
is contradictory, alluring, and painful in the postapartheid South African
psyche. Everything is there: the shattered dreams of youth, sexuality and its
unpredictable costs, AIDS, xenophobia, suicide, the omnipotent violence
that often cuts short the promise of young people's lives, and the Africanist
understanding of the life continuum that does not end with death but flows
on into an ancestral realm. Infused with the rhythms of the inner-city
pulsebeat, this courageous novel is compelling in its honesty and its broad
vision, which links Hillbrow, rural Tiragalong, and Oxford. It spills out
the guts of Hillbrow—living with the same energy and intimate knowledge
with which the Drum writers wrote Sophiatown into being." — Provided by
publisher.
 ISBN 978-0-8214-1962-5 (pbk.)
1. City and town life—South Africa—Fiction. 2. Hillbrow (Johannesburg,
South Africa)—Fiction. I. Title.
 PR9369.4.M68W45 2011
 823'.92—dc22
                                                      2011000719

'Motho ke sera seo fela se rego ge se rakeletšwe se lahle
marumo se hlabane ka leleme . . . '
*A human being is a beast that when cornered throws
away weapons and fights with the tongue . . .*
(O K Matsepe)

'Reader, be assured this narrative is no fiction.'
Mmadi, tseba gore kanegelo yekhwi ga se nonwane.
(W E B du Bois)

To my friend and former teacher, Sr. Mary Anne Tobin.
Mary Anne, may you grow to be as big as an elephant!

Contents

Introduction

GHIRMAI NEGASH

Phaswane Mpe (1970–2004) was one of the major literary talents to emerge in South Africa after the fall of apartheid. A graduate in African literature and English from the University of Witwatersrand, Johannesburg, he was a novelist, poet, scholar, and cultural activist who wrote with extraordinary commitment and originality, both in substance and in form. His intellectual honesty in exploring thematic concerns germane to postapartheid South African society continues to inspire readers who seek to reflect on old and new sets of problems facing the new South Africa. And his style continues to set the bar for many aspiring black South African writers.

Mpe's writing is informed by an oral tradition particular to the communal life of the South African pastoral area of Limpopo. This, in addition to his modern university liberal arts education; his experience of urban life in Johannesburg; and, ultimately, his artistic sensibility and ability to synthesize disparate elements, has marked him as a truly "home-grown" South African literary phenomenon. It is no wonder that the South African literary community was struck by utter shock and loss in 2004 when the author died prematurely at the age of thirty-four. In literary historical terms, Mpe's early death was indeed a defining moment. In an immediate way, his South African compatriots—writers, critics, and cultural activists—were jolted into awareness of what the loss of Mpe as a unique literary figure meant for South African literary tradition. In terms of his legacy, it was also a moment of acute revelation that the force and form of his work was a motivating influence for, just as it was inspired by, the emergence of many more writers of considerable talent. To celebrate Mpe's role as transformative for South African literature is not to make an overstatement. In his book *Words Gone Two Soon* (2005), Mbulelo Mzamane, one of South Africa's literary dons, has the following to say about Mpe's influences and literary interchanges as he considers Mpe and Sello Duiker:

> There was mutual admiration between Duiker and Mpe. Duiker delivered a moving eulogy at Mpe's memorial service. . . . From the outpouring tributes to both, it soon became

apparent, first, that they commanded a considerable following and, second, that among
their peers there are numerous closet scribes
with major stories to tell [about the postapartheid era]. (xii, xi)

Commenting on Mpe's unique writerly contribution
to the continuum of black African literary tradition,
the writer and philosopher Antjie Krog observes:
"For a long time I have been wondering whether a
strong communal sense would have an influence on
the telling and writing of stories in black communities." To have a Western-centered notion of storytelling means, she says, to rely primarily on coherent
linearity, on the presence of a main narrator and a
main story line, and on a proper beginning and end
(56). Answering her own rhetorical question, she
points out that Mpe remains committed to traditional African forms of narrative that allow him, in
his novel *Welcome to Our Hillbrow,* not only to move
in and out of the "physical and the metaphysical
sphere[s]" effectively but also to employ a communal
mode of narrative continuity. The story that begins
with "an opening narrator who dies halfway through"
is carried on by "another narrator [who] takes over
without any obvious change in style or view" (57).

First published in 2001, seven years after South
Africa's liberation from the apartheid system, *Welcome to Our Hillbrow* provides its readers with sub-
stantial criticism and social commentary regarding
the lingering and evolving problems of a new South

Africa. It focuses on themes that Mpe often referred to as "taboos" or "sensitive issues." After a synopsis of the novel's plot, this brief introduction will address the underlying thematic concerns of Mpe's book by grouping them under the conceptual categories *euphemism*, *linguicism*, and *xenophobia*. Of course, the novel's many concerns cannot be reduced to these few groupings. For example, it is evident that Mpe was interested in experimenting with the South African novel as a genre, appropriating traditional or local techniques to tell a contemporary or modern South African story of the postapartheid era. A reader will recognize that in Mpe's text the *what* (narrative representation) and the *how* (language) are blurred entities; the "question of language" is openly a matter of contention; and the challenging social issues extend to other, bigger realms—including the subjects of history, memory, AIDS, linguistic and human rights, and the difficulties of building a globally oriented multicultural nation. But it is fair to say that the themes of euphemism, linguicism, and xenophobia appear as the author's central concerns in the novel.

Plot

The plot of *Welcome to Our Hillbrow* is built around the parallel and intersecting lives of two articulate young black people, one male and one female. It is set in Hillbrow, one of Johannesburg's violence-ridden suburbs, and focuses on the thoughts and activities of Refentše, the central male character, and Refilwe, his female counterpart and one-time lover. Both are budding authors who can write in European and African languages, and their proficiency holds great promise. However, their dreams of leading meaningful lives of intellectual and literary creativity are thwarted as they become victims of literary sidelining and, later, of AIDS. When the novel closes we hear, through echoes and flashbacks, Refentše's voice speaking to us from the other world. At the same time, we see Refilwe returning home from Oxford, England. Before her encounter with other African students in Europe, Refilwe had been a bearer of xenophobia directed against black Africans, who are derogatorily referred to in the novel as the *Makwerekwere* (a slang term of uncertain origin). Having met and fallen in love with a Nigerian student in England, a young man whom she has planned to marry, Refilwe has undergone a transformation and no longer harbors prejudice against other Africans by the time she returns to South Africa. She has embraced a pan-African identity and has hoped to build a family. Her homecoming, however, is marked by tragedy: she has contracted AIDS, and she is returning home to die.

Euphemism and Linguicism

The motif of euphemism becomes central in the novel as Mpe demonstrates how the apartheid state of South Africa managed to keep the black population under its control. As is only too well known, the apartheid state's policy and practice of subjugation of the African masses was instituted in material violence: spatial separation and alienation based on skin coloration; physical detention; the suppression and infiltration of resistance and revolt; the dispossession of land and the eviction of indigenous peoples, followed by their economic exploitation as workers in domestic households, commercial farms, and mineral mines—workers who often led isolated lives secured by what Jonathan Crush calls "panoptical surveillance" mechanisms (832). Also, as Antjie Krog makes clear in her harrowing account *Country of My Skull* ([1998], 2002), the South African state gradually transformed itself into a parasitical paramilitary machine. Given that his South African audience needs no explanation of the material foundations of apartheid, in *Welcome to Our Hillbrow* Mpe does not dwell on apartheid's material exploitation and violence. According to Refentše, the novel's hero, the strength of apartheid lay rather in its ability to make many Africans continue to believe its racial supremacist assumptions. Exploiting black Africans' economic dependency, political apartheid systematically worked to manipulate, as Ngugi would say, the "mental universe" of the black populations in order to prevent their thinking about their victimhood (*Decolonising the Mind*, 16). Thus, in one of the most forceful passages of the book, Mpe shows how life in apartheid South Africa became not only brutal but also unreal and confusing as the black populations that had been driven away from their original spaces were programmed (and coerced) to accept their euphemized spaces as true homes. The novel's narrator says,

> The woman of your fiction, Refentše, was writing in 1995, one year after the much acclaimed 1994 democratic elections; one year after the overthrow of the political and cultural censorship, and of the damaging and dishonest indoctrination system which had been aimed at forcing South Africans to believe that life's realities lay exclusively in euphemisms. These spaces called euphemisms . . . became homelands; where any criticism of Apartheid thinking became a threat to public morals; where love across racial boundaries became mental instability. (57)

This passage brings to the forefront the refutation of the black culture's right to exist by the controlling other. This denial had been normalized and internalized to the extent that multiracial and multicultural fraternization and love had become a source of shame in the public sphere of life. Readers will discern from other passages that the power structure of apartheid denied recognition to the history and existence of rural and urban indigenous culture and its political and cultural heroes. For example,

South Africans wishing to join the system had to accept their marginalized identities, including living in cities whose named components served as constant reminders of their subjugation. As the first chapter, "Hillbrow: The Map" (swarming with European icons and images), leaves no doubt, the street naming became what Ngugi wa Thiong'o describes as "a clear case of conquerors writing their own memory on the landscape of [South African] resistance memory"; the history of the black and nonwhite majority was systematically wiped out (*Something Torn and New,* 113–14). Moreover, in the dichotomous constructions of the apartheid system, all white was good and all black was bad, and black migrants who wanted to receive education or to have better jobs were expected to reject their native ways of life and language in exchange for the "civilised status" maintained by appropriating white characteristics and culture (Jackson, 222).

However, from several other passages in *Welcome to Our Hillbrow*, it is also apparent that it is not merely the remains of apartheid against which young South African men and women must fight and assert themselves today. The central character's story reveals that even after the fall of apartheid and the ANC's ascension to power in South Africa, it was difficult to gain access to, reclaim, and make use of South Africa's indigenous culture and languages. Refentše's stories and the juxtaposed accounts of Refilwe are highly significant in this regard. Their

stories acknowledge that the ideological marginal-
ization and practical neglect of indigenous African
languages and literatures were not and are not the
fault of apartheid alone. The clearly stated reality
that the two characters have to abandon writing
in the Sepedi language because they are unable to
make a name for themselves by writing in an African
vernacular shows the limitations and failings of the
postapartheid state, which seems powerless to put
African vernaculars to effective use. This acknowl-
edgment is vital because, as Refentše laments while
alluding to the predicament of those who write fiction in local languages, South African writers who
want to publish in African languages face a curious
dilemma. While, on the one hand, the opportunity
of writing in African languages has been guaranteed
in the new South African constitution, on the other
hand, writers have come to realize that these languages and literatures are viewed as inferior by their
own reading public. It appears that, by and large,
the indigenous languages and literatures have effectively become the victims of an almost irrevers-
ible phenomenon, which linguist Kwesi Kwaa Prah
(after Phillipson) calls "linguicism." Prah suggests
that the process of linguicism is set in motion when
languages are crowded out, or killed, by the effects
of domineering languages—and when that process,
instead of being corrected, is reinforced through the
validation of "ideas, rationale, structures and prac-
tices which are employed to justify and legitimise

the production and reproduction of resources and power differentials between groups defined on the basis of language and language use" (19).

In the novel, the ramifications of this kind of linguicism are captured in Refentše's memories as he meditates on the risks and limitations of experimenting with African-language fiction. He writes:

> You, Refentše, had written the story of your fictitious scarecrow heroine in an attempt to grapple with these profound questions of euphemism, xenophobia, prejudice and AIDS, to which Tiragalong pretended to have answers. Your story was in English, since unlike the naïve and hopeful woman of your fiction, you knew the limitations of writing in Sepedi. But, like your heroine, you wrote your story in order to find sanctuary in the worlds of fiction that are never quite what we label them. You wrote it in order to steady yourself against grief and prejudice, against the painful and complex realities of humanness. (59)

To a significant degree, this is a continued legacy from the past. In South Africa, black populations have been essentially cut off from their linguistic heritage, particularly in the public space in institutions such as schools, the workplace, and government. Historically this separation has produced conflicting responses from the affected communities.

In *Welcome to Our Hillbrow*, Mpe—through his male character's voice—talks about why writing in an African language actually matters to writers, and why it is feared and resisted by the African elite and the publishing establishment. Through the evocation of artistic images and notions of beauty and a native literary value system, Mpe suggests opportunities where African-language literature could become a "sanctuary" of freedom for the individual and also a contribution "to important discussions of life in South Africa" (58). Yet he makes clear that the literary needs of such writers have been, to a large extent, in conflict with mainstream literary enterprise. In practice, this has meant that they could publish their work when they met the limitations set by censors and publishers but were rejected whenever the latter thought those limits had been transgressed. The supposed transgressions have involved matters of content, style, diction, or, as the novel points out, anything that relates to "morality," however "questionable" and contentious it might be (58). The writer Refentše describes what happened to his peer, Refilwe:

> She did not know that writing in an African language in South Africa could be such a curse. She had not anticipated that the publishers' reviewers would brand her novel vulgar. Calling shit and genitalia by their correct names in Sepedi was apparently regarded

as vulgar by these reviewers, who had for a long time been reviewing works of fiction for educational publishers, and who were determined to ensure that such works did not offend the systems that they served. (56)

Refentše goes on to reveal the contradictions and ironies contained in this practice:

These systems were very inconsistent in their attitudes to education. They considered it fine, for instance, to call genitalia by their correct names in English and Afrikaans biology books—even gave these names graphic pictures as escorts—yet in all other languages, they criminalised such linguistic honesty. . . . In 1995, despite the so-called new dispensation, nothing had really changed. The legacy of Apartheid censors still shackled those who dreamed of writing freely in an African language. Publishers, scared of being found to be on the financially dangerous side of the censorship border, still rejected manuscripts that too realistically called things by their proper names—names that people of Tiragalong and Hillbrow and everywhere in the world used every day. (56, 57)

The use of euphemism is also seen in the representation of AIDS. The disease is viewed as a mysterious and mythical ailment. Rather than being named and explained, it is whispered about, evoking images reminiscent of the Zulu film *Yester-day* (2004), written and directed by Darrell Roodt. In the film, the frightened Zulu villagers go after the infected heroine and her dying husband, who are said to be suffering from a bizarre disease. In *Welcome to Our Hillbrow*, the urban district of Hillbrow and the rural village of Tiragalong compete in mystifying and denying the existence of the "strange illness" (3) while community members point fingers at anyone but themselves as the source of the problem. In this way the affected "other," the AIDS victim, remains euphemized and thus unseen. But however hard one may try to conceal the truth—and this is Mpe's point—the disease is not restricted to rural or urban areas but rather cuts across cities, regions, race, gender, and professions; the AIDS pandemic eventually harms everyone in its way.

Xenophobia

The discussion of AIDS is linked to the issue of xenophobia in the novel. Unable and unwilling to accept the real causes of AIDS, the South Africa of Mpe's fiction largely believes that the *Makwerekwere*—especially the Nigerians—are the bringers of the AIDS disease and immorality. This group of African immigrants and refugees is charged with promiscuity, drug dealing, and violence. Xenophobia also finds expression in other ways. In one example, Refentše's own mother denies the existence of her son's relationship with Lerato, who is black but is considered inferior because of her impure African-ethnic pedigree (39–40). A second example pertains to Refentše's death. It is clear that Refilwe's "carefully re-written version" of his suicide is given more credit mainly because she plays upon the xenophobic beliefs of the community (43–44). In yet another example we are told that although "there were exceptions" (54), the inhabitants of the rural setting of Tiragalong celebrate when a person commits suicide or when a damaging person is eliminated violently from the community—because it justifies their hatred of other Africans and urban dwellers. "Tiragalong danced because its xenophobia—its fear of and hatred for both black non-South Africans and Johannesburgers—was vindicated" (54). The revelation of one xenophobic story after another goes unchecked until Refilwe—once an enemy of foreigners—falls victim to AIDS and returns from Oxford to die in her home village. This moment also contributes to the resurgence of an "always already present" yet long-hidden truth within the community. As Refilwe and her community learn the hard way, the sufferers of AIDS are not foreigners alone, and the existence and impact of AIDS can no longer be ignored by the inhabitants of Tiragalong. Thus, Refilwe's homecoming brings all the xenophobic prejudices surrounding AIDS and the mystification of the disease to the community's attention, and Mpe's narrative is brought to a close.

For those who read a work of fiction primarily for the pleasure of reading, seeing Mpe's *Welcome to Our Hillbrow* as a brilliant linguistic construction of the imagination will be satisfying enough. Of course, Mpe's novel is a literary-aesthetic rendition or refraction of both real and imagined realities of postapartheid South Africa, and it should, first and foremost, be read as such. But for those who want to examine South African society critically, and who seek to understand more and to "reflect on old and new sets" of problems challenging the New South Africa, one of the questions to be asked is this: What do the stories of the characters in the novel tell (or not tell) us about the hopes and dilemmas of postapartheid South Africa as it struggles to transition from a bitter history of apartheid to a democratic, unified, and stable multicultural and multiracial society? As we have seen, Mpe's novel also opens up an opportunity to raise questions and to think through South Africa's positioning within Africa—particularly in its treatment of African migrants. Equally pertinent are questions regarding the status of African languages and their future. All of these issues are important and do matter in South Africa. Yet despite the novel's attention to problems of euphemism, linguicism, and xenophobia, which were at the height of their crisis when Mpe wrote this book about a decade ago—and which continue today with differing intensities—it is also vital to step back and to remember that South African society is a dynamic and resilient society with a distinctive historical capacity for transformation, as is attested by the struggle of its people against apartheid and by the undaunted spirit of resistance of its principal leaders, such as Nelson Mandela. Ultimately, then, the wisdom embodied in Mpe's novel is that in registering serious problems that can explode if left unacknowledged and unattended it provides an appealing catalyst for open debate and resolution via a commonly shared responsibility of South Africans. And with regard to a wider vision of his craft, one may do well to give Mpe the final word:

> My vision is to contribute to a critical engagement with, and [make an] artistically sound contribution to, reflections on sensitive issues in South African literature and society. This is important for the sake of fighting against complacency, as well as providing an antidote to those who think that [we] South Africans have nothing to write about in the post-Apartheid context. (Mzamane, 42)

Works Cited

Crush, Jonathan. "Power and Surveillance on the South African Gold Mines." *Journal of Southern African Studies* 18, no. 4 (1992): 825–44.

Jackson, Shannon. "Coloureds Don't Toyi-Toyi: Gesture, Constraint and Identity in Cape Town." In *Limits* to *Liberation after Apartheid: Citizenship, Governance and Culture,* edited by Steven L. Robins, 206–24. Oxford: Currey; Athens: Ohio University Press; Cape Town: David Philip, 2005.

Krog, Antjie. *Country of My Skull: Guilt, Sorrow, and the Limits of Forgiveness in the New South Africa.* 2nd ed. Cape Town: Random, 2002.

———. "What the Hell Is Penelope Doing in Winnie's Story?" *English in Africa* 36, no. 1 (2009): 55–60.

Mzamane, Mbulelo Vizikhungo, ed. *Words Gone Two Soon: A Tribute to Phaswane Mpe and K. Sello Duiker.* Pretoria: Umgangatho, 2005.

Ngugi wa Thiong'o. *Decolonising the Mind: The Politics of Language in African Literature.* London: Currey; Portsmouth, NH: Heinemann, 1986.

———. *Something Torn and New: An African Renaissance.* New York: Civitas-Basic, 2009.

Prah, Kwesi Kwaa. "Going Native: Language of Instruction for Education." In *Language of Instruction in Tanzania and South Africa (LOITASA),* edited by Birgit Brock-Utne, Zubeida Desai, and Martha Qorro, 14–34. Dar-es-Salaam: E & D, 2003.

Hillbrow: The Map

If you were still alive, Refentše, child of Tiragalong, you would be glad that Bafana Bafana lost to France in the 1998 Soccer World Cup fiasco. Of course you supported the squad. But at least now, you would experience no hardships walking to your flat through the streets of Hillbrow – that locality of just over one square kilometre, according to official records; and according to its inhabitants, at least twice as big and teeming with countless people. You would remember the last occasion in 1995, when Bafana Bafana won against Ivory Coast and, in their jubilation, people in Hillbrow hurled bottles of all sorts from their flat balconies. A few bold souls, boasting a range of driving skills, swung and spun their cars in the streets, making U-turns and circles all over the road. You would recall the child, possibly seven years old or so, who got hit by a car. Her mid-air screams still ring in your memory. When she hit the concrete pavements of Hillbrow, her screams died with her. A young man just behind you shouted:

Kill the bastard!

But the driver was gone. The traffic cops, arriving a few minutes later, found that the season of arrest had already passed. Most people, after the momentary stunned silence of witnessing the sour fruits of soccer victory, resumed their singing. *Shosholoza . . .* sounded its melodies from Wolmarans Street, at the fringe of the Johannesburg downtown, to the head of Clarendon Place, at the boundary of the serene Parktown suburb. *Shosholoza . . .* drowned the choking sobs of the deceased child's mother.

Welcome to our Hillbrow! you heard one man say to his female companion, who was a seeming newcomer to this place of bustling activity, visiting it for the first time since the conspiracy between her parents and fate decided to usher her presence onto the face of the Earth.

Welcome to our Hillbrow . . .

Your first entry into Hillbrow, Refentše, was the culmination of many converging routes. You do not remember where the route first began. But you know all too well that the stories of migrants had a lot to do with its formation. By the time you left Tiragalong High School to come to the University of the Witwatersrand, at the dawn of 1991, you already knew that Hillbrow was a menacing monster, so threatening to its neighbours like Berea and downtown Johannesburg, that big, forward-looking companies were beginning to desert the inner city, heading for the northern suburbs such as Sandton. The lure of the monster was, however, hard to resist; Hillbrow had swallowed a number of the children of Tiragalong, who thought that the City of Gold was full of career opportunities for them.

One of the stories that you remember vividly was of a young man who died of a strange illness in 1990, when you were matriculating. The migrants said it could only have been AIDS. After all, was he not often seen roaming the whorehouses and dingy pubs of Hillbrow? While his poor parents imagined that he was working away in the city, in order to make sure that there would be a huge bag of maize meal to send back for all at the homestead. The migrants, most of whom insisted that he was a stubborn brother, who suffered because of blocking his ears with gum while they dished out advice to him, also said that he was often seen with *Makwerekwere* women, hanging onto his arms and dazzling him with sugar-coated kisses that were sure to destroy any man, let alone an impressionable youngster like him.

He died, poor chap; of what precisely, no one knew. But strange illnesses courted in Hillbrow, as Tiragalong knew only too well, could only translate into AIDS. This AIDS, according to popular understanding, was caused by foreign germs that travelled down from the central and western parts of Africa. More specifically, certain newspaper articles attributed the source of the virus that caused AIDS to a species called the Green Monkey, which people in some parts of West Africa were said to eat as meat, thereby contracting the disease. Migrants (who were Tiragalong's authoritative grapevine on all important issues) deduced from such media reports that AIDS's travel route into Johannesburg was through *Makwerekwere;* and Hillbrow was the sanctuary in which *Makwerekwere* basked.

There were others who went even further, saying that AIDS was caused by the bizarre sexual behaviour of the Hillbrowans.

How could any man have sex with another man? they demanded to know.

Those who claimed to be informed – although none could admit to having seen or practised it personally – said such sex was done anally. They also explained how it was done – dog style – to the disgust of most of the people of Tiragalong, who insisted that filth and sex should be two separate things.

Surely, this large group argued, it was the shit that the greedy and careless penises sucked out of the equally eager anuses, that could only lead to such dreadful illnesses?

Such were the scandalous stories that did the rounds on the informal migrant grapevine.

For formal news, there was Radio Lebowa – now Thobela FM – broadcasting snippets of car hijackings and robbers' shoot-outs with the Johannesburg Murder and Robbery Squad every news hour. Five men were found with their ribs ripped off by what appeared to have been a butcher's knife . . . Two women were raped and then killed in Quartz Street . . . Three Nigerians who evaded arrest at Jan Smuts Airport were finally arrested in Pretoria Street for drug dealing . . . Street kids, drunk with glue, brandy and wild visions of themselves as speeding Hollywood movie drivers, were racing their wire-made cars through red robots, thus increasingly becoming a menace to motorists driving through Hillbrow, especially in the vicinity of Banket and Claim Streets . . . At least eight people died and thirteen were seriously injured when the New Year's Eve celebrations took the form of torrents of bottles gushing out of the brooding clouds that were flat balconies . . . Men going anywhere near the corner of Quartz and Smit Streets were advised to beware of the menace of increasingly aggressive prostitutes . . . a few men had allegedly been raped there recently . . .

Welcome to our Hillbrow . . .

And, of course, television added its lustre to the radio snippets. Crime was glamorised on the screens and robbers were portrayed as if they were movie stars. Heroes of grimy courage and exceptionally vicious greed were followed by the voracious camera lenses of modern technology, and the little boys of Tiragalong emulated their TV heroes, driving their cars made of wire with wheels of tennis balls.

Vum . . . vum . . . and beep . . . beep . . . their cars went in the streets of Tiragalong.

Then you arrived in Hillbrow, Refentše, to witness it all for yourself; and come up with your own story, if you could. You came to be a witness, because your cousin, with whom you were going to stay until you found student accommodation at the University, stayed in Hillbrow, although not exactly in the centre of the action. For he did not stay in the main streets, Pretoria and Kotze, nor in the somewhat notorious Esselen, all of which run parallel to each other. No! He did not even stay in the most notorious Quartz Street – joining the three at right angles – which is what people often mean when they say:

There is Hillbrow for you!

If you are coming from the city centre, the best way to get to Cousin's place is by driving or walking through Twist Street, a one-way street that takes you to the north of the city. You cross Wolmarans and three rather obscure streets, Kapteijn, Ockerse and Pieterse, before you drive or walk past Esselen, Kotze and Pretoria Streets. You will then cross Van der Merwe and Goldreich Streets. Your next port of call is Caroline Street. Just cross to the other side of Caroline. On your left-hand side is Christ Church, the Bible Centred Church of Christ, as the big red letters announce to you. On your right-hand side is a block of flats called Vickers Place. You turn to your right, because the entrance to Vickers is in Caroline Street, directly opposite another block, Da Gama Court. If you are not too lazy, you will ignore the lift and walk up the stairs to the fifth floor, where Cousin stays.

So far, you have not seen any car chases or witnessed a shoot-out. You did meet some semi-naked souls whom your guide, from the same village of Tiragalong, called prostitutes. Otherwise, the thing that stands out in your memory is the extremely busy movement of people going in all directions of Hillbrow, seeming to enjoy the neon lights of the suburb, while others appeared to be in a hurry to get to work – or, yes, to *work*. Now, you were not in a position to say what *the work* was. You knew, though, that a student's guide to careers in South Africa would probably not have listed it as an entry. It amazed you that there should be so many people jostling one another in the streets at nine in the evening. When did they prepare their meals and go to sleep?

Vickers Place struck you as a fairly quiet building. You never expected any quietness in our Hillbrow. But then, Caroline Street, where Vickers was situated, was not at the centre of Hillbrow. The centre was Kotze Street, where OK Bazaars shared the pavement with the rather quiet pub, *The Fans*, and the louder one, *The Base*. Cutting across Kotze at right angles was Twist Street. Enclosed by Twist and Claim Streets, Kotze and Pretoria, was Highpoint, the biggest shopping centre in Hillbrow. That was where Clicks, Spar, CNA and other stores were housed. It was in this centre that you would find Standard Bank, with its cash machines flashing 'Temporarily Out of Service', on Sundays and public holidays, as well as on weekdays after eight in the evening. Trying to save you from being mugged? Possibly; but, in the process, forcing you to use at extra cost either First National Bank's autoteller, at the corner of Twist and Pretoria, or ABSA Bank's machine, just across Kotze. Caroline Street was not visible from this vantage point. Nor was it near Catherine Avenue, the boundary of Hillbrow and Berea, where Checkers competed for our financial attention (when we had any) with what appeared to be a terribly noisy shebeen, *Jabula Ebusuku*; which in turn competed for our spiritual commitment with its neighbour, the Universal Kingdom of God. There was an added benefit to Vickers's particular location. Another branch of Spar was just two streets away, at the corner of Caroline and Claim Streets, so you could buy your groceries and other necessities there. Tied into an embrace with Spar was *Sweet Caroline*; not Neil Diamond's piece of music, but a different kind of tune – a bottle store – which soothed the exhaustion and taste buds of Hillbrowans living in this part of our world. The concrete pavements here, like those of the inner Hillbrow, teemed with informal business, in the form of bananas, apples, cabbages, spinach and other fruits and vegetables; good-looking produce at low prices that rendered the buying of such produce from Spar, Checkers or OK ridiculously wasteful. True, Quartz Street ran close to Vickers. Indeed, it was the very first street to the east of Vickers, and there was more bustling activity in Quartz than in either Caroline itself, or Twist and Claim. However, the fact of being almost on the outskirts of the inner Hillbrow appeared to have rendered this part of Quartz more harmless and pleasurable – to the extent that anything in Hillbrow could be either of these things – than the sections deeper in the suburb.

The quietness endured for the better part of the night. Your cousin, after feeding you well, left you alone to go to bed because you cried about exhaustion. Your guide left with him too. They were going to see Hillbrow, they said. You slept in your cousin's bed. Fell asleep despite your anxieties.

Will they come back? you asked yourself initially. Will robbers break into the flat? And if they do, what will I do?

Sleep caught you, gently; caught you while you drifted in and out of these Hillbrow anxieties, with your memory constantly jogging back to Tiragalong with such nostalgia that one would have thought you had not been there for at least a year.

Then you shuddered into wakefulness. You tried to convince yourself that the sound you had heard was a dream, a nightmare; but in your wakeful state, hard realities came home to roost. A second gun shot rang in Twist Street, and you remembered Tiragalong with stronger nostalgia than you had ever imagined to be possible. A woman screamed for help. Police sirens went off loudly. You realised a few minutes later, from the fading sounds, that they were going to rescue someone else, elsewhere, and not the nearby screaming soul whose voice continued to ring relentlessly. You were tempted to jump out the bed and peep out of the window, but you decided against the idea. Instead, you tried to nurse yourself back to sleep.

Welcome to our Hillbrow . . .

You were struck by the quietness of Vickers and its immediate surroundings. And now, as you gradually fell back to sleep, it was the screams of human voices and police sirens that surged up from the depths of your sleep into the nightmares and dreams of your first night in Hillbrow. That was on the Sunday at the dawn of January 1991.

The following day you woke up, washed yourself thoroughly; quite a treat. Water being such a scarce resource in Tiragalong, you only used to take a proper bath once a week. Sure, there were taps at most street corners in Tiragalong. But the water taps were often as dry as a desert. So here you received a treat; warm, hot and cold water right in the flat. You left the bathroom feeling fresh enough to be able to approach the officers of the big University without worrying that your presence might be somewhat offensive to their sense of smell.

Your cousin had phoned his supervisors to let them know that he might be late for work. He would be taking his cousin, who had just arrived in Johannesburg for the first time, to the University to register.

So for the first time, you see Hillbrow in the splendour of sunrays. Your own and Cousin's soles hit the pavements of the Hillbrow streets. You cross Twist, walk past the Bible Centred Church. Caroline makes a curve just after the Church and becomes the lane of Edith Cavell Street, which takes you downtown; or, more precisely, to Wolmarans at the edge of the city. Edith Cavell runs parallel to Twist. Enclosed within the lane that runs from Wolmarans to Clarendon Place (which becomes Louis Botha a few streets on) is a small, almost negligible triangle of a park. On the other side of the park, just across Clarendon Place, is Hillbrow Police Station, in which you take only minimal interest. Crossing the park, you walk alongside the Police Station, still in Clarendon Place. A very short distance later, you join Kotze Street. In Kotze you turn right to face the west. Cousin stops you.

If you want it, he says wryly, you can go into this building.

He points to a building at the corner of Clarendon Place and Kotze, the entrance of which is in Kotze. It is called Quirinalle.

Or if you prefer, you can head on to the very end of Kotze, he continues. You see those green, yellow and red lights dancing? That is Chelsea.

One semi-naked soul comes out of Quirinalle and Cousin's point is made. So you do not ask him, as you had meant to, what *it* was.

Now we are heading for Braamfontein, Cousin intimates.

Almost immediately after turning right into Kotze, you stop at a traffic light; Hospital Street, you read. The robot goes green and you cross.

We are now in Braamfontein, I think, Cousin says. I never really know whether Braamfontein begins here or in the next street.

On your right-hand side you see what looks like a

rather big dog kennel. Although you note it, it does not strike you as an important object. Except that, un-announced, a young man crawls out of it, smoking dagga and dealing glue some severe blows. And singing very loudly and well – at least the voice has what you would call a melody, although the logic of the lyrics eludes you. Further on, about fifty metres from the head of Kotze, you see some old people, about fifteen of them, sitting against a cream and brown wall. Cousin tells you that they are beggars. But they do not beg anything from you and Cousin. They simply continue to mind their own business. Then, as you draw level with the last of them, he shouts:

Aibo!

Cousin ignores him. You wave your hand at him.

Ngiyabonga Baba, he returns your greetings with a smile.

Hey you! You do not go around greeting every fool in Hillbrow. He looks harmless. But not all people who greet you in Hillbrow are innocent well-wishers.

He looks very grimy. Out of his mouth come strong whiffs of methylated spirits. And spittle drools down his dirty beard onto his bony chest. His trousers are inclined to intimate that urine has gone through them quite a number of times. He leans against the wall more steadfastly, seeming satisfied with your response.

As you come to the head of Kotze, you cross Joubert Street Extension, where Kotze begins its jour-ney into the heart of Hillbrow, turning left along the wall of the Civic Centre – now Metropolitan Centre –

and then right, as if you are going to enter the building. You walk through the passage that goes through the Civic Centre into Loveday Street, which runs parallel to Joubert Street Extension. You cross the street. On your right-hand side, you are greeted by a black glassy structure called Civic Theatre. You walk past that, on a pathway that runs between it and another park. You ignore the people playing soccer in the park, paying no attention at all to the way their shoes menace the lovely lawn. At the end of the park, you cross Simmonds Street. You go straight on, and you are now in Stiemens Street.

This takes us straight to the University, Cousin informs you.

From what you had heard about Braamfontein, you never imagined that you would find all these dirty children, occupying themselves by taking turns at glue. But here they are. You cross Biccard Street, which, as you learn, takes you straight into the city. And then Melle, De Beer and Bertha. You turn right into Bertha. A few metres ahead is a robot. On the wall, a metre or two from the traffic light, you read: University of the Witwatersrand, Johannesburg, 1 Jan Smuts Avenue. So Bertha becomes Jan Smuts, and the street making a T-junction at the robots is Ameshof. For the first time, you see the headquarters of the South African Breweries, 2 Jan Smuts Avenue, opposite the University.

Not a bad couple, knowledge and relaxation, you muse.

You walk up the stairs in Jan Smuts Avenue. You enter the University premises. The dull greyness of the

University's buildings announces the gravity of what people do here. All the buildings you see around you are grey. First, the Ernest Oppenheimer Life Sciences and the Old Education Building opposite it, and then the Physics Building and what you later learn is the Wartenweiler Library opposite it. And then the giant structure that you often see in pictures of the University, the Central Block. You do not claim to have a well-developed appreciation of architecture. But you wonder how any University with Architecture as one of its specialities, as you read in their information booklet, could allow such huge but ugly structures to be erected on its premises.

When you get to the Central Block, Cousin asks around, twice, for Senate House. The second time he is successful. You are there, really. It is a building adjacent to the Central Block. You go into the giant structure, ask again for directions to the Central Admissions Office. You find a helpful senior student who, instead of giving directions, opts to take you there. So this is the Central Admissions Office. The officers in the Central Admissions Office send you from one office to another, until Cousin's time runs out. He whispers with you, and you agree that yes, you have seen the way – and sure, you can find your way back without a problem. So he leaves for work. And you remain, to sort out your future with the University officers and your lecturers-to-be.

On your way home to Vickers, at the cream and brown wall of Usindiso City Shelter, you again respond to the old man's *Aibo*! Again, he thanks you for your generosity. You are persuaded to search your trouser pockets for a cent or two . . .

This procedure is one that is to repeat itself many times for the rest of that year. Coming as you do from a poor family, you do not have enough money to pay the required deposit for student accommodation. Your applications for bursaries have not been successful, for although you passed your Matric with the necessary exemption to be admitted to read for the degree of Bachelor of Arts, the organisations you applied to for financial assistance required that applicants' Matric results should be more than sparkling. So it was that you had to stay with Cousin at Vickers Place for the whole of 1991, and subsequently. Your tuition fees, as well as the cost of your books and other study materials, were covered by rather hefty study loans. The loans increased in number and size during the subsequent three years. At the end of 1994, you passed your degree of Bachelor of Arts, Honours, with distinction. It was only after that, in 1995, that you were awarded a scholarship to see you through the degree of Master of Arts. It was with this scholarship that you settled your student accommodation account at Parktown Village. People said you were extremely fortunate. The generous ones agreed that you deserved your good fortune. For, in January 1996, as soon as you had completed your postgraduate degree, you were taken on by the University as a lecturer, without having to suffer any period of unemployment.

It was during your second month as lecturer that

you saw your friend from the shelter being wheeled away in a wheelbarrow, in the direction of Hillbrow Hospital in Klein Street. He did not say *Aibo!* this time. This pained you. In the five years you had known him, you had become friends without ever saying anything to each other, except for the mutually warm greetings.

Now, on this day of Bafana Bafana's defeat in 1998, had you, Refentše, still been alive to witness it, you would probably not have been too sorry, despite your passion for soccer generally and your love for Bafana Bafana specifically, that they had lost. Because now it would be easy for you to make your way home to our Hillbrow from your University office in Braamfontein. You would be able to move without hurry along the pavements of Kotze and other streets. You would make a detour, as was your habit, into your favourite pub, *The Fans*. You would probably not be sufficiently moneyed to order Guinness draught, so you would settle instead for the popular Castle Lager, the South African Breweries lager which, the adverts claim, *has stood the test of time.* People would still be talking about how sad it was that so-and-so missed a penalty:

A gift from the gods, really, that penalty, one would say.

While another might insist that the French goalkeeper was simply too good for any Bafana Bafana striker.

Your nose, Refentše, would have caught the scents and aromas of such talk ever since your entry into Kotze Street. Since you had not watched the match yourself, you would refrain from commenting too strongly. However, the news of Bafana Bafana's defeat would be no surprise to you, because Lerato, aware that you were working your health away in the office, would have called at the first opportunity to greet the Bone of her Heart and to give you an update on the match.

You would immediately have pictured Cousin's disappointed face at the result. Like most Hillbrowans, Cousin took his soccer seriously. You and he had had many disagreements on the subject of support for foreign teams – especially those from elsewhere in Africa. You often accused him of being a hypocrite, because his vocal support for black non-South African teams, whenever they played against European clubs, contrasted so glaringly with his prejudice towards black foreigners the rest of the time. Cousin would always take the opportunity during these arguments to complain about the crime and grime in Hillbrow, for which he held such foreigners responsible; not just for the physical decay of the place, but the moral decay. His words were echoed by many others – among them, the white superintendent at your place in Van der Merwe Street, who told you when you moved in that Hillbrow had been just fine until those Nigerians came in here with all their drug dealing.

You, Refentše, child of Tiragalong (and, as you insisted in the days just before your death, also of Hillbrow), had never shared such sentiments. It was your opinion that the moral decay of Hillbrow, so often talked about, was in fact no worse than that of Tiragalong.

Think about it, Cousin, you would challenge. How

many people are here in Hillbrow? How many of them are criminals? If you consider that the concentration of people in Hillbrow is dense, and work out the number of crimes in relation to the number of people, I tell you, you will find Tiragalong to be just as bad.

Anyway, there are very few Hillbrowans, if you think about it, who were not originally wanderers from Tiragalong and other rural villages, who have come here, as we have, in search of education and work. Many of the *Makwerekwere* you accuse of this and that are no different to us – sojourners, here in search of green pastures. They are lecturers and students of Wits, Rand Afrikaans University and Technikons around Jo'burg; professionals taking up posts that locals are hardly qualified to fill. A number of them can be found selling fruit and vegetables in the streets, along with many locals – so how can they take our jobs? Of course there are some who do drug trafficking. But when the locals are prepared to lap at them like starved dogs, what do you expect the struggling immigrants to do?

And while we're so busy blaming them for all our sins, hadn't we better also admit that quite a large percentage of our home relatives who get killed in Hillbrow, are in fact killed by other relatives and friends – people who bring their home grudges with them to Jo'burg. *That's* what makes Hillbrow so corrupt . . .

You would want to add that some *Makwerekwere* were fleeing their war-torn countries to seek sanctuary here in our country, in the same way that many South Africans were forced into exile in Zambia, Zaïre,

Nigeria and other African and non-African countries during the Apartheid era. You would be reminded of the many writers, politicians, social workers and lecturers, and the endless string of South Africans hanging and jumping from their ninth floor prison cells because the agents of the Apartheid government wanted them to do so. The latter was called *Learning to Fly*. You would also remember the grisly details, draped in tears, from the testimonies of the Truth and Reconciliation Commission hearings, of South African policemen enjoying their beer and braai while black dissenters roasted alongside their roasted meat in the heat of a summer day – stuff that would be called surrealism or magic realism or some other strange realism were it simply told or written as a piece of fiction. And of course you could not forget all those black agents of the Apartheid State, playing their various roles with a mastery that confounded the minds of even the State itself. Black police officers contorting bribes from fellow blacks accused of political and other dissents. Black police and security forces hitting fellow blacks mercilessly for crimes that were often not committed . . . *Teaching the kaffir a lesson or two*, as they said.

You would usually, however, spare Cousin these historical details, since he knew them just as well as you did; or rather, much better than you did, since he himself was part of the interrogating police force that knew only one reliable way of accessing truth from suspects: *torture*. Cousin would interrupt your thoughtful silence, by reminding you that you were ignoring more pressing concerns. Like the AIDS that *they* transport into the country.

Ah! This AIDS nonsense! I wish those girls and boys in our villages had more respect for their genitalia and did not leave them to do careless business in Hillbrow, only so that we can attribute the source of our dirges to Nigeria and Zaïre and . . .

Cousin would not agree with you, of course. He never agreed with you where black foreigners from African countries, vulgarly referred to as *Makwerekwere*, were concerned. *Makwerekwere* was a word derived from *kwere kwere*, a sound that their unintelligible foreign languages were supposed to make, according to the locals. Cousin insisted that people should remain in their own countries and try to sort out the problems of these respective countries, rather than fleeing them; South Africa had too many problems of its own.

Surely we cannot be expected to solve all the problems of Africa? he would insist.

You agreed that we could not, even if we tried. But then, that was no excuse for ostracising the innocent, you also said.

Cousin would merely snort, fingering the gun buckled onto his waist belt.

The difference between you and Cousin was that he was a policeman. If *you* had no problems with *Makwerekwere*, then that was fine. What could you do anyway, even if you despised them with every drop of the river of blood and other juices that flowed in your body? On the other hand, being a policeman, there were many things that Cousin could do. And he did them . . .

It was true that the beer you enjoyed was often bought by Cousin. And the food. You were, despite your disapproval of his actions, a beneficiary of his activities. Like so many people were beneficiaries. Including the close relatives and friends of his colleagues. Together with his colleagues, he would arrest *Makwerekwere*. Drive them around Hillbrow for infinite periods of time.

See it for the last time, bastards, they would tell the poor souls.

When the poor souls pleaded, the uniformed men would ask if they could make their pleas more visible. They did. Cousin and his colleagues received oceans of rands and cents from these unfortunates, who found very little to motivate them to agree to be sent back home. Some of the womenfolk bought their temporary freedom to roam the Hillbrow streets by dispensing under-waist bliss. They preferred to eke out a living here. Yes, they were ostracised, they agreed; but when the police left them in peace, they could gather a thing or two to send back to their families at home. The foreign exchange rate really did favour them.

The *Makwerekwere* had also learned a trick or two of their own. Get a member of the police, or a sympathetic South African companion, to help you organise a false identity document – for a nominal fee. Or, set up a love relationship of sorts with someone from the city. It was better, so the word went around, to be so related to one who worked in *the kitchens*, as white suburbs are often referred to – the reason being that most black people eking out a living there were women doing kitchen and other household work (if, that is, one discounted the lovers and prostitutes engaged in bedroom work with the wealthy masters and madams). Police bothered you less often in the suburbs, because those were not regarded as high crime zones. And the security personnel who guarded those kitchens were often more preoccupied with chasing real criminals than people who simply came there to visit their friends and loved ones.

Which is not to say that these kitchens were absolutely safe. As you, Refentše, know so well!

The first time someone took out a knife on you, it was at Hyde Park Village, near Sandton, where you accidentally disturbed thieves stripping cars of their radio sets in the parking lot; Hyde Park, with its lily-white reputation for safety and serenity. You were not stabbed, but only because you made it just in time into the courtyard of your aunt's employer's house, and the butcher knife pursuing you hit the door to the court-yard just as you turned the key to lock it.

You also liked to quote the story of how you and your University mates were held at gunpoint at Parktown Village in June of 1995, while a Wits University car that one of the students had borrowed was successfully redistributed. All the time that you and your friends were lying there, flat on your stomachs, people were jubilantly singing *Amabokoboko ayaphumelela* . . . in the streets, because the South African rugby team, the Springboks, had just won the Rugby World Cup.

There were other chilling stories of what happened

in the kitchens. Of white madams raped and gagged by their South African garden boys – that is, black men to whom they could not afford to show any respect; of white men found hanging like washing waiting to dry, because they refused their so-called boys and girls permission to go home to bury a close relative; of whites killed simply because they were wealthy and tried to protect their wealth when robbers came to redistribute it; of whites hacked to death simply because they were white, an embodiment of racial segregation and black impover-ishment, irrespective of their political allegiances and economic affiliations.

These are examples of the many cases of crime not caused by *Makwerekwere*, who were at any rate too much in need of sanctuary, even if it was sometimes a cold one, to risk attracting the attention of police and security services. *Makwerekwere* knew they had no re-course to legal defence if they were caught. The police could detain or deport them without allowing them any trial at all. Even the Department of Home Affairs was not sympathetic to their cause. No one seemed to care that the treatment of *Makwerekwere* by the police, and the lack of sympathy from the influential Department of Home Affairs, ran contrary to the human rights clauses detailed in the new constitution of the country. Am-biguities, paradoxes, ironies . . . the stuff of our South African and *Makwerekwere* lives.

Your mind, Refentše, would no doubt drift on in this fashion until, looking at your wrist-watch, you would wake up sharply to the fact that it was now late. The food that Lerato would have prepared would be getting cold. You would exit the pub without ceremony, rush off to your flat in nearby Van der Merwe Street, where the inviting smell of delicious food would be assaulting the nostrils of those passing along the corridors. And your Beauty would be waiting patiently for your arrival.

Lerato, the Bone of your Heart, to whom you opened your heart a day after the robbery at Parktown Village. She had been part of the victimised group. The incident had shaken you badly, made you think about the possibility of your joint deaths occurring before she could learn that you loved her. You made up your mind, firmly, to declare yourself to her the following day. Just in case there should be another robbery and that this time the robbers should be in a hurry to kill. When you finally did open up your heart to her, with many misgivings about the possibility of rejection, Lerato had looked at you and said, without mincing her words:

Coward! You could have said something long before today!

When she kissed you to demonstrate her point, you were left in no doubt that this was not the usual kiss of a friend, such as she often gave you. Yours was a long-standing friendship, that you had established over a period of two and a half years as fellow students in the University; a friendship, that is, that had stood the test of time. You kissed each other again. And that was how it came about that, when you rented this flat in Van der Merwe Street, you decided to invite Lerato to stay with you.

Now, Refentše (had you still been here to continue your habits of living), now would be the time for you to rush home to find your Lerato. Your heart would be glowing with warmth that increased with every step you took. You would be reminded of all the other occasions on which you had rushed home with just such a sense of eager haste, never anticipating the treachery to come; never imagining, not for a moment, that fateful morning when you arrived home unexpectedly to find Lerato minding a lover's business with Sammy, your mutual friend.

The shock of that discovery had caused your mind to sink into its swamp of melancholy. With Stimela's *See the World through the Eyes of a Child . . .* providing the musical background to your brooding, you sat alone on your twentieth-floor balcony, thinking your gloomy thoughts about love, friendship and the whole purpose of living . . .

And when you finally come to this part of your journey that ends in the blank wall of suicide . . . with the spinning of cars the prostitution drug use and misuse the grime and crime the numerous bottles diving from flat balconies giving off sparks of red and yellow from mid-air reflections of street and flat neon lights only to crush on unfortunate souls' skulls the neon welcoming lights the peace of mind you could see in many Hillbrowans the liveliness of the place and places collapsing while others got renovated new concrete and brick structures standing up where you thought there was no longer any space for anything Quirinalle Hotel changing names and you hoped activities to Badiri House Chelsea Hotel closing down robbery moving flowing from Hillbrow into its neighbours especially Berea and Braamfontein as the media had it *Mail & Guardian* and David Philip Publishers and others changing offices moving out of this increasingly dilapidated and menacing Braamfontein while others found it to be quite an investment and so coming in to build and occupy their lush offices the Department of Home Affairs moving from downtown Johannesburg into Braamfontein and *Makwerekwere* drifting into and out of Hillbrow and Berea having spilt into Berea from Hillbrow according to many xenophobic South Africans and their glamorising media and into Braamfontein to sort out their refugee affairs and the streets of Hillbrow and Berea and Braamfontein overflowing with *Makwerekwere* come to pursue green pastures after hearing that the new president Rolihlahla Mandela welcomes guests and visitors unlike his predecessors who erected deadly electric wire fences around the boundaries of South Africa trying to keep out the barbarians from Mozambique Zaïre Nigeria Congo Ivory Coast Zimbabwe Angola Zambia from all over Africa fleeing their war-torn countries populated with starvation like Ethiopia flashing across Cousin's TV screen every now and then *Makwerekwere* stretching their legs and spreading like pumpkin plants filling every corner of our city and turning each patch into a Hillbrow coming to take our jobs in the new democratic rainbowism of African Renaissance that threatened the future of the locals Bafana Bafana fans momentarily forgetting xenophobia and investing their hopes in the national team whose entry into the World Cup was its first attempt in such matters the fans also investing in the Moroccan team the Nigerian Super Eagles and singing at least they are African unlike the French the English the Danes and all that jazz and xenophobia revisited through images of Philip Troussier the Bafana Bafana coach as a sinister Frenchman come to ensure that his country wins the Cup by crippling the South Africans . . .

All these things that you have heard seen heard about felt smelt believed disbelieved shirked embraced brewing in your consciousness would find chilling haunting echoes in the simple words . . .

Welcome to our Hillbrow . . .

Notes from Heaven

If you were still alive now, Refentše, child of Tiragalong and Hillbrow, you might finally have written the books you had hoped to write; completed your collection of poems called *Love Songs, Blues and Interludes*, that you wished to dedicate to our Hillbrow. Your one published short story about life in Hillbrow might have paved a smooth way to more such stories. You often used to think about the scarcity of written Hillbrow fictions in English and Sepedi. You asked around, and those who could read the other nine of the eleven official South African languages answered you by saying that even in those languages, written fictions were very scarce.

How does it happen that Hillbrow is so popular, but writers ignore it? you asked.

Oh! I think it is too notorious for them to handle, an acquaintance had answered one day.

They never saw enough of Hillbrow to be able to try to write about it, another suggested.

You were forced to shrug your shoulders. Nobody appeared to have a convincing answer. But then you had found a mission in all this omission – a mission to explore Hillbrow in writing. A mission to produce at least one novel, or a semblance of one, based on your impressions of Hillbrow. You made what you initially thought was a bad beginning when your attempt to write the novel resulted in a short story. You contemplated whether to continue trying or not. When, in September of 1995, your short story was accepted for publication in a reputable literary magazine, you wondered whether it was not better to write more of the same, and perhaps later rework them into a novel, which you could then translate into Sepedi. You had thought about these things, child of Tiragalong and Hillbrow; but not with the same conviction that you had thought about suicide.

As you look back now at your life on Earth, you find it grimly amusing that suicide could be so seductive. You are fascinated by the stories of your home boys and girls, talking about your suicide as if no thought had gone into it, their stories moving with ease to and from Tiragalong and Hillbrow and all the other corners of the Gauteng Province where fellow villagers are to be found. It was minibus taxis and migrants' cars that transported the news. It was Telkom's telephone lines that performed a similar function. It was Vodacom and MTN, South Africa's giant cellphone service providers. And credit must be given, too, to the villagers' abilities to imagine well beyond the known and the possible, in order to embellish the story of your suicide.

One of the chief embellishers was Refilwe, your sometime Tiragalong girlfriend, with whom you parted company when you discovered that she had at least four other love relationships ongoing. It was when you began to teach at the University that Refilwe reappeared in your life. She came to Hillbrow at the dawn of 1996, having just completed her degree of Bachelor of Arts, Honours, in Sepedi and English, at the neighbouring University of the North, at Mankweng, twenty-five kilometres north of Pietersburg. She had come to Johannesburg to seek green pastures for herself and those she loved. She phoned you at work to say that she needed a testimonial. She had applied for the post of Assistant Editor at one of the Johannesburg publishing houses. Besides two testimonials from her lecturers, she explained to you, her prospective employers required a third one from someone who knew her as a member of the same community.

But why me? you had asked, worried that you were probably not the most appropriate person to write her a testimonial.

You see, Refentše, I know why you ask that question. Because we were in love and things turned out negatively, you think you cannot say much for me.

But there are things you can write, really. I am sure that you know me well enough to look beyond the now-ruined kraal of love that we had once made our shelter. Besides the fact that I believe that your kind-heartedness would not blind you to the positive aspects of my being, your testimonial, coming from an educated person, is likely to carry more weight than if it came from some-one else.

You mused; that was probably true. It was rather unfortunate to be uneducated, because people took you less seriously in such matters. You mused some more, then said:

All right, I shall try something.

You did not have to try too hard. Refilwe, as you knew, was a hard worker. She had done exceptionally well at school as well as in her University studies. She was a kind-hearted and generous soul. Her open-thighedness was the only side of her generosity that you did not like. For that you could not blame her too strongly, though, you yourself having subsequently committed the sexual error that you never imagined you could commit at that time when you judged her so strongly, after your remarkable discovery of her infidelity. You also reasoned that her sexual life would not hinder her from doing her work. It never did. That was why she had done so well in her studies. So the strokes you made on your computer keyboard resulted in the following:

REFILWE MAGETLA: A TESTIMONIAL

This serves to confirm that I know Ms Refilwe Magetla.
Ms Magetla lives in the same village as myself, and she
matriculated through the same school, Tiragalong High,
that I attended.

What stands out about Ms Magetla is her appetite
for learning and capacity for hard work. I first observed
this significant streak of her personality at Tiragalong
High in 1991, when I did voluntary library work for
the school. She visited the library often and consist-
ently. With her capacity for hard work, I was not at all
surprised when she applied to study at the University
of the North in 1992. Despite coming from a rather
disadvantaged educational background, Ms Magetla has
coped extremely well at the University, as her first class
passes in her major subjects testify.

As a person, Ms Magetla is very friendly and easy
to get along with.

Refilwe did get the post. And phoned to thank you most
heartily. Because you were so happy for her and you still
loved her somewhat, despite your separation, you
suggested that you meet in the flesh in order to
congratulate her. She found you enjoying a lager in
Sweeney's in the Braamfontein Centre, just opposite the
University of the Witwatersrand. You spent the late af-
ternoon together, separating when Lerato arrived to walk
home with you, as arranged.

You did not know what was going on in Refilwe's
mind that day, except that she was happy. You were to

learn the rest a few weeks later. She phoned and said she would like to see you again, at her tiny bachelor flat at Vickers Place. At her tiny flat, because she wanted to cook for you, to remind you that she was still Refilwe.

Well, you thought, there was no point in rejecting the invitation, although you would have preferred to meet her elsewhere. You were all too aware that being alone with her might lead to a point where you would begin to wonder whether you had been justified in separating from her at all; she who had begged for your forgiveness. Surely, in her act of betrayal, she had merely done what all human beings are capable of doing? You knew you did forgive her – in the sense that you had no desire to take revenge by betraying her in turn. But you had left her anyway, because, at the time, you thought that it was absolutely despicable to be so sexually loose. You hardly considered that your sudden departure was, in its way, also an act of betrayal; betrayal of her faith in your capacity to forget and live happily ever after with her. A betrayal of your ability to say:

You are just a mere mortal, Refilwe. I am sure you will learn your lessons like all of us.

You had since had occasion to rethink your self-righteousness. That was when you yourself made love with your friend Sammy's lover (Sammy who, just ten months later, would ironically come to betray you in turn). The incident had taken place during the May of 1995 – the year that preceded Refilwe's reappearance – just before the start of your love life with Lerato. You had never planned it. You did not even imagine you could do it, until it happened.

Sammy had had a fight with the Bone of his Heart on that day. The woman, Bohlale, had phoned you. She asked you to come and listen to her story. When she told you how Sammy came in drunk, with a *Lekwerekwere* woman that he had picked up from Chelsea, and instructed Bohlale to sleep on the floor, you had expressed a great deal of sympathy. You wondered how Sammy could behave like that. He was certainly not a violent man. Nor was he a womaniser. Bohlale had agreed with you. But she pointed out that he had taken strange drugs. She did not remember ever before coming across the kind of smell that Sammy's breath shot at her that night. The whore he came in with boasted openly that she had put something in his drink while he was busy dancing. Sammy, enjoying his moments of heavenly bliss in his singular drunkenness, said and did nothing to contradict the whore, nothing to try, even if in vain, to put Bohlale's heart at rest.

You know that I love him, Refentše. But I must be suspicious of a man who wastes his time in Chelsea. How can we live together? Just think about it. If I keep quiet, he will do it again. And it was important for me to make a noise in front of that bitch, so that she too would know that there is at least one woman who will not tolerate this shit.

Sammy, for his part, was never able to tell the full story, because he did not know it himself. He remembered that he started drinking with the woman in *The Base*. She was just a woman with whom he happened to share a table. He excused himself to go to the toilet, and on his return had only taken a few sips from his glass of beer, when blackout caught up with him. To be overcome by blackout was a rare event for Sammy, he who could drink like a fish and still remain mentally and physically erect, like a stubborn tree trunk defying angry storms.

Refentše, child of Tiragalong and Hillbrow, you had looked at Bohlale with a sympathetic gaze, your eyes contracting as you tried to understand what could have taken Sammy to Chelsea, which he actually despised. You remembered what Oom Schalk Lourens of Herman Charles Bosman's short stories had to say, about some things simply baffling the human mind, even the most agile of human minds. You had come to sit closer to Bohlale. You had looked into her eyes. Her shattered emotions made you feel extremely close to her. You even remembered that you might have been lovers in your high school days, had it not been for the fact that you could not open yourself to her then because at that time she was in love with another classmate.

Let me talk to Sammy, you suggested, and find out what this thing is about. I am sure he still loves you. Only earlier in the day I was with him. We parted when I went to *The Fans*. He was going to see a friend in Berea. I'm surprised that he ended up in Chelsea, the place that he abhors so much. But be strong for now Bohlale. Of course both of us know how much he loves you!

Bohlale's heart swelled with this generous expression of sympathy and support. She began to sob softly. You gave her a hug, an embrace. The spiritual support had to be backed up by a physical one. You knew well enough that physical touch could work wonders. You yourself always felt better when a friend gave you a hug, a pat on the shoulder – something like that – when you were sad, hurt or even when you had achieved. So you did what you liked friends and close, caring relatives to do for you.

Bohlale returned your sympathy with a hug, an embrace of her own.

The boy in your trousers decided to express his sympathies too. You felt your heart begin to beat quite fast. Gentle drops of sweat began to do the rounds on your back. Your dilating eyes sent a subtle message of love to Bohlale, although you would have tried harder – had you only known how – not to send such a message. It was, in its intention, an innocent message, but the conscience of friendship required that it should rather not be sent.

Bohlale's heart was receptive to your unintentional message. She held onto you a bit more tightly. Squeezed your hand. Gave it a gentle scratch in the centre of its palm. The last blow to your self-control happened when you landed a kiss on her full lips . . .

And so, with this memory in mind, you would have preferred on this day not to visit Refilwe at her flat. Because you knew how weak you could be. Of course, you were not a womaniser. That act of betrayal with Bohlale was the first and last sexual betrayal you ever committed. You had no intention now of betraying Lerato and – who knew? – perhaps Refilwe's lover as well. Did she have one? From your knowledge of Refilwe, she probably had at least one.

The more you thought about her, the more you found your thoughts turning to Lerato. You left work early on the day of the arranged meeting. Not because you wanted to meet Refilwe ahead of time. No. You left early, because you wanted to go home first. To see Lerato. To have your fill of her kisses and embraces to strengthen you, the way powerful leaders get *dingaka* to strengthen them with medicines. You needed to remind yourself that someone called Lerato was at home, waiting patiently for the Bone of her Heart to come. This time and all times. You did not wish Refilwe to be the one to welcome you to our Hillbrow when you came from work.

You could not anticipate, not having eyes to see into the future, how futile your efforts at fidelity were to be. But not because of any betrayal on your part. You had no way of knowing that within a few short weeks of this day, you would find Lerato and Sammy minding their lovers' business in your bed. Nor could you guess the tragic chain of events that would follow from this painful discovery.

Love. Betrayal. Seduction. Suicide. It was such things as these that you might have written about, Refentše, child of Tiragalong and Hillbrow, had you not chosen to exit prematurely from this world of trials. You know what a seductive subject suicide can be. Because when it seduced you, you found nothing in life to pull you away from the seduction. You had quarrelled with your mother because you insisted on being in love with

Lerato, a Hillbrow woman – as Tiragalong insisted on labelling her. Your efforts to explain that she was from Alexandra, a black township about twelve kilometres north of Johannesburg, did not help to ease your mother's relentless hatred for this Hillbrowan that she had not even met yet. She despised her, because your trusted female cousin had told her that, judging by the way you no longer cared for or about anyone from Tiragalong, it was absolutely clear that Lerato had spiced your food and drinks with I-am-the-only-one, the strongest love potion known in Tiragalong and beyond. Your mother knew that all Hillbrow women were prostitutes, who spent their nights leaning against the walls of the giant buildings in which they conducted their trade of under-waist bliss; their human thighs, pasted against the brick-work, serving as both advertisements and sexual commodities. Your mother had never been to Hillbrow, nor to any part of Johannesburg. But mi-grants – some of whom possessed storytelling skills that could imprint the most vivid images on a person's mind – told these stories with relish. A significant number of them happened to be shoppers themselves. But your mother was not interested in such details. She hated the Hillbrow women with unmatchable venom – a human venom so fatal it would have put the black mamba's to shame.

When you went home two weeks after pay-day, and you had nothing to give your mother, because your salary was not enough to settle your study loan repay-ments and other accounts and still leave you with anything to spare, it was confirmed in your mother's mind that you were indeed a victim of the cunning of the Hillbrowans. The result was that when you found your Lerato and Sammy moaning together in your bedroom that morning, your enthusiasm for life got badly shattered. This was partly because you had invested too much faith in Lerato, as if she was incapable of committing the same deeds that you had committed. And it was partly because you could not now go to cry on your mother's shoulder. You knew she would say:

I told you!

She had, indeed, told you. That if you did not part from Lerato, you were no longer your mother's son. Since you had not listened, you must now face the consequences alone. Equally, how could you turn for comfort to your friend-turned-traitor, Sammy? And since love, friendship and motherhood did not provide any possibility for sanctuary in your hour of need, you began to look increasingly at the positive sides of suicide. You looked until you found them. *Relief* was the sum total of the benefits you discovered. Relief from the pressure to succeed, with the weight of Tiragalong's expectations on your back. Relief from the constant financial strains and burdens. From the unending disappointments of life etched on your brain, with your mother, friend and lover as some of their embodiments. And relief too from your nagging sense of guilt over your own betrayal with Bohlale, from whom you had parted in the enmity of quarrel and whose sudden shocking death had cheated you of the chance to reconcile. There were no outlets for your bottled-up feelings. You rarely discussed your private life with other people, and those to whom you might have confided your troubles were the very ones who were the source of your pain. With so much on your mind, *suicide* and *relief* could only be synonymous attractions. Suicide could be as seductive as Bohlale lying there on the bed, in need of your companionship. As seductive as Lerato must have been to Sammy; although you never discovered exactly how both came to be involved in this love life of theirs. Because you jumped from the twentieth floor of your building before you could find out.

Refentše, child of Tiragalong and Hillbrow, wel-come to our Hillbrow of milk and honey and bile, all brewing in the depths of our collective consciousness . . .

Refilwe, your old girlfriend who still loved you, despite all the water that had passed under the bridges between you, did not have a full understanding of your complex misery. Aside from your personal achieve-ments – the fact that you were the first person from Tiragalong to obtain the degree of Master of Arts at the University of the Witwatersrand, or indeed any other University; that you were a lecturer and a prospective writer, who already had one story published – you looked happy enough. Refilwe could not know any differently, because you confided nothing to her. So she had no idea of the conflicts you were going through. As far as she knew, there was only one person to blame for your prematurely wasted life. When, after your death, the people of Tiragalong bad-mouthed you, when they said that you did not care about your own mother – Poor woman! – Refilwe would come to your defence. She said of course you cared. Everyone knew what a caring individual you had been. Look at your voluntary library service at Tiragalong High. Look at the way you helped those people, like herself, who needed written testimonials. It was inconceivable that you could love and care for everyone except your own mother. But Refilwe's eloquence on your behalf was not impartial enough. She remembered too well that day when she had invited you to her flat, when you had more than disappointed her. You had thought at the time that she understood your reasons for refusing her tempting charms. Which she did. But she also understood that she had every good reason to draw your heart's attention from Lerato. That was why her testimony about you, when she went home about two months after your burial (her schedule did not allow her to be part of the mourning procession), was so destructively seductive. She sent you hurtling towards your second death. She blemished your name more than anyone else could have hoped to do. Her tongue was a generous flow of milk, nourishing Tiragalong with stories of your intellectual achievements, coupled with your sad emotional naïveté. It was this naïveté that had allowed you to get hooked up with the Johannesburg woman who was your final nemesis. Had you only been less naïve, Refilwe implied, you would have foreseen how that story was to end. You would not have walked into such a trap in the first place.

Refilwe rewrote large chunks of the story that

Tiragalong had constructed about you, which was that you committed suicide because your mother had bewitched you. In an attempt to drive your heart from the Johannesburg woman, Tiragalong had said, your mother had used medicines that were too strong. They destroyed your brain. Twisted its thinking and made you see life as a hideous monster clawing you to death, trying to get a grip on your heart. Tiragalong's story was constructed when your mother slipped and fell into your grave on that hot Saturday morning of your burial. As Tiragalong believed, only witches could fall into a corpse's grave on burial. Medicine men had confirmed that, in the good old days, such things only happened to witches after they had bewitched the deceased; either because their medicines were too strong for their victims to die alone, or because the gods became angry and vented their wrath on the witches. So the Comrades of Tiragalong, in order to cleanse the village, had necklaced your mother to death. They put large tyres round her neck and poured generous quantities of petrol onto them and onto her whole body. Then someone gingerly lit a cigarette before throwing the match into her hut, in which she awaited the Second Coming of our Lord. The match flame died only after a fruitful interaction with the petrol. Huge flames blazed up and caught the thatch of the hut.

Refilwe could not rewrite the death of your mother; but she rewrote the version of your suicide. In this version of things, you had been bewitched indeed – but not by your mother; by a loose-thighed Hillbrowan called

Lerato. Tiragalong's bias against Hillbrow women enabled the ink of her tongue to be galling. Her story did not lead to anyone's physical death; only the death of your reputation was the fruit of her careful farming methods.

Tiragalong drank in the scandal eagerly; of course, it agreed with her, everyone knew that Johannesburg women were bound to bring disasters upon any man's life.

But worse still, the woman is not even a Johannesburger, Refilwe had intimated. I hear from reliable sources that her mother comes from Durban. But her father is a Nigerian, who fled his war-torn country. The two of them met in Alexandra, where the mother lives. Apparently, the mother had been struggling somewhat. She lived on lice, so to speak. So she was quite happy to find this Nigerian. You know *Makwerekwere*! When they love you, they simply dish out all these monies they have to you. Drug-dealing being such a business, you can always be sure to be well off with a Nigerian man . . .

And so Refilwe's vengeful story continued. With very little regard for hard facts. With rumours and imaginings taken for valid testimony. And your suicide taken for hard evidence of the dangerous power of *Makwerekwere* women. Nobody in Tiragalong knew then that Lerato's father was not, in fact, the Nigerian, but Piet, who was also Tshepo's father. The story only came out long after your and Lerato's suicides. It was told to your youngest cousin by Lerato's younger sister, with whom your cousin was then in love. Tiragalong was shocked to learn that the despised Lerato and the beloved Tshepo were, in fact, sister and brother.

Tshepo, your friend and role model, had been the first person in Tiragalong to go and study at the University of the Witwatersrand. Tshepo was the one who encouraged you to act on your dreams of higher education and writing success. You had never really got over his untimely death, after he was struck by lightning in January 1991, just after receiving his University degree. His mother, on hearing the news of the calamity, choked to death on her grief. Because, as they say, a corpse is always de-skinned on someone else's back, Tshepo's neighbour, one of the oldest women in the village, was accused of having sent the lightning to strike him.

Sheer jealousy was her motive, Tiragalong had suggested. The suggestion quickly became accepted as valid fact. A bone thrower confirmed that the woman was indeed a witch. She was even said to have bewitched her own husband, as well as her illicit lover, both of whom had died some years previously of mysterious diseases. Mysterious diseases, in Tiragalong's view, could only result from a mysterious cause: witchcraft. It was only after the witch had found her punishment by necklacing, that Tiragalong was given cause to realise its mistake in concluding the book of her life in that manner.

There was no father of Tshepo to be grieved by the loss of so promising a flower. He had died when Tshepo was about four years old, and Lerato's mother, with whom he was conducting his secret affair, was still in her early stages of pregnancy. Lerato was still being nourished and clothed by her mother's placenta when her father was knifed to death in Alexandra, for reasons that were best known to his knifers. They were reasons that nobody in Tiragalong could imagine. All Tiragalong could say, when it learned of the event, was:

We thought it was just the younger generation that was a problem. But clearly, fathers are just as lost as their children. What is becoming of the world these days . . . ?

In any event, Refilwe's version of things provided good diversion for a large section of Tiragalong's story-loving population. Opinions were divided as to whether her version was true or not. Some said it didn't matter, that whether you died because of a *Lekwerekwere* or a Johannesburger did not make much difference. Were the two not equally dangerous? Immoral . . . drug dealing . . . murderous . . . sexually loose . . . money grabbing . . .

Others said: What a pity that Refentše's mother had to pay the price for loose Hillbrowan sins; her intentions clearly were noble, her only mistake being that she used medicines that were too strong in her attempts to save him from himself. It is, after all, a mother's responsibility to hold the sharp edge of a knife, so that her baby does not stab itself with it.

At least one person, though, knew better. At least one person knew the extent to which all the versions were false. And this person, because she knew better, found the thought of suicide to be just as seductive as you, Refentše, had found it; as seductive as the words you spoke to her on the day that you finally opened your heart to her, following the robbery at Parktown Village. This person brooded with increasing gloom about that day of bliss. And she brooded even more about that other occasion, the anything-but-blissful day on which your unanticipated return caught her open-thighed, with your friend Sammy moaning on top of her . . .

You did not know how that part of the story had come about. Had you known, you would perhaps have forgiven your Lerato, instead of taking that spectacular route to the world of the Ancestors. You have since come to learn the facts, because Heaven affords you the benefit of retrospect and omniscience. Heaven, you now know, is not some far-off place where God sits in judgement, waiting to read out his endless, cruel list of offenders on Earth. This Heaven that is your present abode is a very different thing. It carries within it its own Hell. You understand now that you are, in fact, a killer. You killed yourself. And unintentionally, you have also killed your own mother. You are a killer, Refentše, child of Tiragalong and Hillbrow. Because of your initial act of killing, Heaven has afforded you an opportunity, not only to watch your screaming mother follow you – her neck draped with huge tyres wet with petrol, melting in the heat of the roaring flames – but also of watching Lerato decide to follow in the footsteps of the Bone of her Heart. Heaven affords you, too, the opportunity to watch your friend Sammy lose his sanity in the midst of the mental and emotional pressures that your suicide, his lingering grief over Bohlale's death, your mother's necklacing and his own guilt over the part he played in it, bring to bear on his consciousness and conscience. No, Refentše, child of Tiragalong and Hillbrow, you would not have blamed Lerato entirely, had you known the circumstances. You would have preferred to forgive her instead. You would have said to her, with a loving kiss:

Such is the way of heart and flesh, Bone of my Heart.

You would have understood that she and Sammy were as well-intentioned as you were on the day that you and Bohlale betrayed Sammy. You would possibly have gone even further, and opened your heart a little bit more, by telling her, for the first time, that you had committed a similar crime. You had let your heart and semen spill over into Bohlale's heart and womanhood – so full that heart was with love and care! You would have understood that Sammy was, in the same way, trying to save your and Lerato's love relationship, because you had become too frustrated and depressed to maintain it yourself.

The first sign of your growing loss of control occurred after you went home one weekend to Tiragalong. You soon returned, having been told by your mother that you must leave Lerato – leave her, or you were no longer her son. The shocking precision of her words and the determination in her voice had drawn your heart away from Tiragalong. You discovered, on arriving in Hillbrow, that to be drawn away from Tiragalong also went hand-in-hand with a loss of interest in Hillbrow. Because Tiragalong was in Hillbrow. You always took Tiragalong with you in your consciousness whenever you came to Hillbrow or any other place. In the same way, you carried Hillbrow with you always. That day, when Lerato brought you food – she was an outstanding cook – you told her you were not hungry. She knew immediately that things were not right. She was used to you swallowing once or twice more, even when you were already full, just to satisfy her. She did the same for you when you offered her something to bite. Both of you knew only too well that you did not simply disappoint the Bone of the Heart for nothing. When you again refused her food and – the second indication – showed no sign of enjoying the games you often played together, she began to drift into depression. More so because when she asked what was wrong, you said:

Nothing.

Nothing could not be a satisfactory answer when love was crumbling before her eyes. *Nothing* could not bring any radiance to her heart. Nor to yours.

Lerato, that loving child of Alexandra, Tiragalong, Durban and Hillbrow, had called Sammy. To explain to him what she had noticed concerning your loss of appetite for food and love and life. To try and see whether Sammy had any idea of what was bothering you. And to investigate whether she or Sammy could do anything to make your life more liveable. They ended up doing exactly what you and Bohlale had done in your attempt to make Sammy and Bohlale's lives more liveable. And you, child of Tiragalong, when you found them in the midst of their moment of ironic bliss, you imagined that the betrayal had been going on for a long time. Imagined Sammy waiting for you to go to work and then, as soon as you had left, running to your flat to take a round or two with Lerato, whose Bachelor of Arts with Honours classes only ran in the afternoons, and who was therefore not forced to be on Campus at eight in the morning.

You had let your imagination explore the limits of its capacity. In this, it did not fail you. It went very far indeed. So far that Lerato and Sammy suddenly became not just traitors, but Devils. But your imagination also clouded your memory, so that you forgot, for the time being at least, the humanness of what they did; the humanness of what you and Bohlale had done – a humanness that could be viewed as human only so long as it remained uncovered by prying eyes and unpublicised by enthusiastic tongues.

The only difference was that with you and Bohlale, Sammy had not found out. He had gone back to Chelsea by that time, as you learnt later. The Chelsea drugs had been too seductive for him to resist. It only took you a short time, with Bohlale's support, to show Sammy that what he was involving himself in was going to destroy not just his love life with Bohlale, but also his life as a whole. Your brotherly and her loverly counselling were lent weight by the night prowlers in Quartz Street. They found Sammy dazed one night, towards the start of his drug-taking career. They beat him up and took all his money. Which, as far as Sammy could remember, was quite a lot. Scars are always a spring of wisdom, as the saying goes. One of the prowlers, who apparently took the saying literally, thought that such fools had to be left with an actual scar. As a reminder of what life in Hillbrow was like. So he had stabbed Sammy in the chest. You, Refentše, saved Sammy because you recognised his screams as you were passing by, on your way from *The Fans*. You called a cab and had him taken to the Johannesburg Hospital in Parktown.

He was quite sober when you arrived at the scene of his bloody river. His vision of looming death was stronger than the drugs that he had swallowed or sniffed or smoked – or a combination of all three. He recognised you as soon as you arrived. His first words were:

Refentše, child of home, where is Bohlale . . . ?

Then his breath faltered, along with his voice. But the most important thing about this question, from your point of view, was that you were able to repeat it to Bohlale, when you returned from the hospital, without being a liar. So Bohlale realised just how much Sammy loved her. When she began to sob, your heart was pained. You knew very well why she began to sob. She had earlier in the day told you that she was leaving Sammy. She had already packed her things when you returned from the hospital to share with her the sad story of what had happened to her lover. She saw her mistake of judging Sammy too sharply. But you also knew that she was thinking of what you had done with her in those moments of mutual support, when you both tried to understand the elusive depths of Sammy's heart and mind. When you both tried to listen to your brains and bodies in order to find out whether they had any wisdom to impart to you.

That same night, Bohlale phoned you at a most unholy hour, around two in the morning. As soon as she heard your concerned greetings, she began to sob. You visualised her face with those tears of pain digging dongas into her beautiful cheeks. As she kept you in suspense with her sobs, you began to fear the worst; that Sammy must be dead! But when she finally spoke, it was to communicate grief of a different kind.

We must confess and apologise to Sammy about what we did! What kind of friends are we, Refentše, who could just lead themselves into temptation like that? What friends betray their loved ones in this manner?

If telephones had cameras and screens on which you could see the image of the person you talked with – as information scientists make us believe we will have in the near future – then Bohlale would have seen you, Refentše, scratching your head gently. Trying to search the numerous, agile tissues of your brain for a suitable answer.

I hear you, Bohlale, you finally said. What kind of friends are we indeed? But this is not the time for such discussions. I wish we *could* simply confess and cleanse our consciences. But it's not that easy. Remember that Sammy is badly injured. The last thing we want to do is to burden him further with the pain that our story will cause. We need to think through carefully what we will say to him. We must wait until he's well before we decide anything.

Bohlale did not agree. Her burdened conscience could not bear the deception a moment longer. She tried to pressurise you into agreeing to tell Sammy the truth at the first opportunity. The two of you ended up quarrelling. And you spent the rest of the night trying to read yourself back to sleep with John Maxwell Coetzee's *Waiting for the Barbarians;* seeing *Confessions* and *Apologies* filling every page that you turned.

As it happened, you were spared the need for decision. Because the very next day Bohlale, on her way to visit Sammy at the hospital, was knocked over by a speeding car that jumped the red robot. It was driven by hijackers fleeing a pursuing convoy of Johannesburg Murder and Robbery Squad cars, with noisy sirens and flashing blue lights signalling the urgency as well as the gravity of the police mission. Bohlale was run over because, although she had made way for the speeding cars, the hijackers had lost control of their newly appropriated vehicle. They ran into her right where she stood on the pavement. After her death, any confession seemed a needless complication. You reasoned that Sammy had enough grief to deal with, without your aggravating it with apologies that would not serve any purpose now.

So the secret of your dealings with Bohlale remained locked in your heart, surfacing to your consciousness now and then, but never finding outlet.

It was partly because of her – to find relief for your heart's load of love and guilt and grief – that you started writing your short story about Hillbrow. It was initially to be about Bohlale – an expression of the love and care you'd felt towards her on that night of your mutual transgression; and of the regret you felt over the bad terms on which you parted just before her fatal accident. But as you started writing it, it turned into something else. It became instead a story about an HIV-positive woman from Tiragalong, who was ostracised by her fellow villagers when they learnt about her health status. The Tiragalong of your fiction said that she deserved what she got. What had she hoped to gain by opening her thighs to every *Lekwerekwere* that came her way? She was a child who had, in effect, committed suicide. And, as Tiragalong well knew, the cry of a person who has committed suicide is a drum; when it plays we dance. So in your story, as in real life, Tiragalong danced because its xenophobia – its fear of and hatred for both black non-South Africans and Johannesburgers – was vindicated.

There were exceptions, of course. Among those who read your story were some who said that your heroine should not be condemned since she was just a worker in the kitchens, whose poverty caused her (as might have been the case with anyone else in her position) to take advantage of the care that potential lovers could bring. These sympathetic ones went further and pointed out that there was no actual evidence to say that she was in love with a *Lekwerekwere*. Anyway, if she was, what was wrong with that? Who said that the people of Tiragalong were cleaner than everyone else? Were there no stories of Tiragalong people who died of sexually transmitted diseases, with genitals so swollen and decaying that one could hardly recognise them for what they were? Villagers who had never been to Jo'burg or any other part of South Africa, and whose sexual experiences were limited to encounters with other villagers. Were the people of Tiragalong really better than anyone else, when there were so many stories of fellow villagers bewitching one another? At least AIDS came by accident, unlike such malicious acts as sending lightning to strike Tshepo. One could not keep on condemning people for diseases that they had not purposefully passed around.

The diseased woman of your story did not resolve to tumble down from the twentieth floor of her building, to escape her misery. She chose a different route to dealing with her life. Her first resolution was to stop going home, to Tiragalong, where the wagging tongues did their best to hasten her death. But then she discovered, like you did, Refentše, that a conscious decision to desert home is a difficult one to sustain. Because home always travels with you, with your consciousness as its vehicle. So her second resolution was to pour all her grief and alienation into the world of storytelling. You had her write a novel about Hillbrow, xenophobia and AIDS and the prejudices of rural lives. Given the limited length of your short story, you could not explore the issues in any satisfactory detail.

You did find occasion to mention, though, that she made a big mistake by writing her novel in Sepedi. Although she worked in the kitchens, she knew English well enough to write in English. It was not for nothing that she was in her third year of the Bachelor of Arts degree at the University of South Africa, accumulating her credits slowly but surely. She was working in the kitchens because Johannesburg did not afford her the opportunities that she was looking for in this city of gold, milk, honey and bile. She was working in the kitchens in preparation for better days in the future, when, armed with knowledge and certificates, she would leave her employers and seek a career.

She did not know that writing in an African language in South Africa could be such a curse. She had not anticipated that the publishers' reviewers would brand her novel vulgar. Calling shit and genitalia by their correct names in Sepedi was apparently regarded as vulgar by these reviewers, who had for a long time been reviewing works of fiction for educational publishers, and who were determined to ensure that such works did not offend the systems that they served. These systems were very inconsistent in their attitudes to education. They considered it fine, for instance, to call genitalia by their correct names in English and Afrikaans biology books – even gave these names graphic pictures as escorts – yet in all other languages, they criminalised such linguistic honesty.

Now, for nearly fifty years, the system of Apartheid had been confusing writers in this way. Trying to make them believe that euphemism equals good morals. That if you said shit, you were immoral and an unsuitable writer for school children, with their highly impressionable minds. The woman of your fiction, Refentše, was writing in 1995, one year after the much acclaimed 1994 democratic elections; one year after the overthrow of the political and cultural censorship, and of the damaging and dishonest indoctrination system which had been aimed at forcing South Africans to believe that life's realities lay exclusively in euphemisms. These spaces called euphemisms, where arid Bantustans – into which hordes of black South Africans were driven according to their language groups (real or imagined) by the agents of the Apartheid system – became homelands; where any criticism of Apartheid thinking became a threat to public morals; where love across racial boundaries became mental instability . . .

In 1995, despite the so-called new dispensation, nothing had really changed. The legacy of Apartheid censors still shackled those who dreamed of writing freely in an African language. Publishers, scared of being found to be on the financially dangerous side of the censorship border, still rejected manuscripts that too realistically called things by their proper names – names that people of Tiragalong and Hillbrow and everywhere in the world used every day.

The woman of your fiction, Refentše, took her writing seriously. Perhaps too seriously. When the reviewers suggested that she tone down her language, she refused. Publishers in turn exercised their right to reject her literary contribution to Sepedi literature. So the story of Hillbrow and xenophobia and AIDS and the nightmares of rural lives remained buried in the heroine's files. Her disappointment was too strong for her. She had thought that she was contributing to important discussions of life in South Africa. She was grieved to discover that good literature was not judged according to artistic beauty and the truth value of what was said. She was dismayed to learn that artistic skill and honesty could be compromised in the name of questionable morality.

Having taken to her novel-writing as a sanctuary from the lashing tongues of Tiragalong, the woman of your fiction became eaten up by grief and bitterness when the sanctuary proved to be too fragile. There was no longer any meaningful mechanism for her to express herself. The rejection slip and the flimsy explanations made an impact that was not flimsy. She degenerated. Those who met her in the city – especially the unsympathetic ones – said that she was so thin, her clothes were simply hanging on her bony frame. She would have made a better scarecrow than the real ones that were kept in their mealie and sorghum fields in Tiragalong, they said.

They did not realise that they were the sources of her scarecrow state. They did not know that they, together with the moralistic guardians of change, were destroying that keen intellect that worked in the kitchens, and that initially had hoped to make a difference to the cultural life of South Africans. And even if they had known, would they have cared? It was probably better, in their estimation, that she faded away. Because she dared to write things that were critical and showed up their prejudices.

You, Refentše, had written the story of your fictitious scarecrow heroine in an attempt to grapple with these profound questions of euphemism, xenophobia, prejudice and AIDS, to which Tiragalong pretended to have answers. Your story was in English, since unlike the naïve and hopeful woman of your fiction, you knew the limitations of writing in Sepedi. But, like your heroine, you wrote your story in order to find sanctuary in the worlds of fiction that are never quite what we label them. You wrote it in order to steady yourself against grief and prejudice, against the painful and complex realities of humanness.

Considering these grave questions from so many different perspectives made you think anew about your own transgression with Bohlale. In your defence, you reminded yourself that you had not gone on that occasion to dish sex onto your plate from a whorehouse. You could not say for sure, however, that you never would do such a thing. After your deed with Bohlale, you had lost part of your self-confidence in these matters. You had learnt that you were as vulnerable as the drunks and womanisers that you used to criticise for their carelessness; as vulnerable as the prostitutes populating Quartz and other streets, pasted against the walls of the concrete towers of Hillbrow.

For all those reasons you would have understood, had you had time enough to reflect on things, how and why it was that Lerato and Sammy had come to do what they did. Perhaps then, you would not have chosen to leave the face of this Earth so spectacularly. Your mother's death would not have followed yours. Nor would the Bone of your Heart have swallowed those numerous, lethal tablets that she decided to swallow after one of your enemies had threatened to inform her mother of her own contribution toward your suicide.

The enemy knew the secret, because guilty conscience had so tormented Sammy that he lost his reason. In his insanity, he had told a fragmented version of the tale of his and Lerato's betrayal of your love and trust. Tiragalong had conveniently pieced the fragments together to build up a story. It was a story with a smooth narrative current, stripped of all rough edges, devoid of any gaps that might suggest good intentions on either one's part. Some said such behaviour was only to be expected of a Johannesburg woman. Others said who could expect any better from a *Lekwerekwere*. Most agreed that it was short-sighted of you to believe that any woman encountered in the city could be a good partner.

Euphemism. Xenophobia. Prejudice. AIDS. You wrote your story to think through all these issues, child of Tiragalong and Hillbrow. But your story was neither long nor sophisticated enough. You realised when it was published that it would never be sufficient. You became keenly aware that no matter what other stories you might write, none of them would ever be sufficient to answer such imponderables. For to have these answers was to know the secrets of life itself. There would always be another story of love, betrayal, friendship, joy and pain to add to your narrative granary. There would always be the need to revise, reinforce, contradict. For every new personal experience adds to our knowledge of life and living, death and dying. Every act of listening, seeing, smelling, feeling, tasting is a reconfiguring of the story of our lives.

Yet, when Lerato and Sammy provided you with the chance to add to your storehouse of experience, you could not rise to it. It was at that point that you began to brood, a tinge too gloomily, about love and friendship and the whole purpose of living. With Stimela's *See the World Through the Eyes of a Child* . . . your favourite song, providing the musical background to your brooding . . .

And so when you finally come to this part of your journey to embracing the seduction of suicide the spinning of cars the prostitution drug use and misuse the grime and crime the numerous bottles diving from flat balconies giving off sparks of red and yellow from mid-air reflections of street and flat neon lights only to crush on unfortunate souls' skulls . . . Bohlale and the Hillbrow child dying as they hit the concrete pavements of Johannesburg Refilwe rewriting the version of your living and dying Tiragalong condemning both you and the Bone of your Heart the scarecrow woman of your fiction stifled by the repressive forces of democratisation and Hillbrow and Tiragalong flowing into each other in your consciousness . . .

If you were still alive now, Refentše child of Hillbrow and Tiragalong, if you were still alive, all of this that you have heard seen heard about felt smelt believed disbelieved shirked embraced brewing in your consciousness would still find chilling haunting echoes in the simple words . . .

Welcome to our Hillbrow . . .

The Journey through Alexandra

Y ou cannot exactly say, Refentše, that you were
happy when Lerato swallowed those tablets. *See
the World through the Eyes of a Child . . .* was
there, providing musical background to the moment
of her reckoning. As you watched her make her final
decision from your heavenly vantage point, you wished
that you could return to Johannesburg and have a chat
with her. Impart to her the understanding that it was
not entirely her own fault, as people had implied, that
you chose to travel that singularly spectacular route of
suicide. You wished you could let her know that your
problems lay in Tiragalong as much as Hillbrow.

You wished that Sammy, too, could have understood these things – that he was not alone in these acts of betrayal, as the conscience of friendship and love insisted on calling them. Had he understood, Sammy would not have felt the need to support the Comrades of Tiragalong when they accused your mother of being a night prowler. He would simply have said:

Yes, she is. And so am I and all of us . . .

And had he understood, Sammy might not have drifted into insanity the way he did.

You regretted, too, that you were not there to defend Lerato against the cruel telephone call from Terror, when he taunted her with the threat that he was going to tell her mother about the part she had played in your suicide. Terror was a fellow villager who held a long-time grudge against you because you had once disagreed with him when he wanted to incite the pupils of Tiragalong to strike against their teachers. His motive was resentment. He had missed school one Friday and refused to accept his assigned punishment for that. Because your classmates respected you and because you presented an eloquent case in which you demonstrated that Terror's intentions were for his benefit alone and nobody else's, you had gained support from your classmates. Which meant that Terror failed to mobilise any for himself. He had never forgotten that insult.

So when Terror first met Lerato, at your flat in Van der Merwe Street, he had immediately thought of making advances to her. Everyone from Tiragalong knew that Terror was a womaniser of the worst kind. Long before your death, he was already making a career for himself as a rapist. He didn't care who he raped. Any vulnerable woman or girl was fair game to him. There were many such vulnerable people in our Hillbrow, where human cries for help often went unanswered, the multitudes passing by as if oblivious to what was happening, afraid to intervene out of concern for their own lives.

Because he was full of spite towards you, Terror wanted to take Lerato's thighs for a playing field, in which his penis would be player, referee and spectator simultaneously. He wanted to be able to say, later:

But what can you tell me now! I have eaten her! She is just as cheap as they all are.

Lerato had told you about his advances. Then, one day, when Terror was on one of those missions of his, trying to convince you in his poisonous way that, having become friends through you, Sammy and Lerato were too close for any caring lover to be comfortable, you had ordered him to leave your flat and not to visit again. You had told him who the unreliable friend from Tiragalong really was; he who could not be trusted with a friend's wife or girlfriend. He whose respect for his manhood was so shallow, that he left it to swim in the pools of AIDS spilling into the night streets of our Hillbrow. Terror had looked at you with eyes that burned with wrath. But he also knew that, although you were gentle, you could fight if you had to defend yourself. So he left you alone, with words to the effect that you would remember him when the right time came.

That was why, when Sammy told the fragments of his story to Tiragalong, Terror had taken the earliest opportunity to phone Lerato, to scare her with the great revelation that her and Sammy's murderous behaviour was known to all in Tiragalong. And that it was about to become known to the people of Johannesburg as well. Beginning with Lerato's own mother, whom Terror was volunteering to go and inform personally. That was why Lerato had swallowed the numerous lethal tablets. With your favourite song, *See the World through the Eyes of a Child . . .* providing the musical background to the occasion. Because it reminded her of you, Refentše, in the good days of your blooming love; and on the fateful day of your staging of the drama of dying. Your music system was found playing that very song on that day.

Lerato was not in a position to face her mother with the truth because she knew her mother loved you. She had said a number of times that you were an ideal son-in-law. Her comments were not just referring to your education and future prospects, though those were no doubt important. She was also full of praise for your personality. Given that she loved and trusted Lerato, she would have found it impossible to believe that her daughter could betray you in that way. When she came home from work one late evening and found Lerato dead, she had painfully assumed that Lerato's heart had been gnawed to pieces by grief at the loss of the Bone of her Heart . . .

Lerato never for a moment considered that her mother would understand her. So she had chosen to follow in your tracks, rather than to yield to Terror's blackmail that if she let him play his games between her thighs, he would keep her secret safe from her mother. Terror's words were madness itself. Lerato hated him and his words with acid hatred. The very thought of opening her legs to him made her choke with disgust. The thought was enough to lead her to the discovery of just how seductive suicide could be. Strengthening her resolve, was the thought of Sammy, basking in the sanctuary of his insanity, while she suffered alone. All alone.

You wished, Refentše, that you could return to Johannesburg to let Lerato know that she was never alone in these acts of well-intentioned generosity that we call betrayal, that you too had tasted their bitter-sweet fruits. But you were powerless. You could not return to Alexandra, where Lerato was staying at her mother's house, when she swallowed the tablets. You could not, because you were not in control of life in this Heaven. Just as you were not in control of life on Earth.

I do not own life, you often said when you tried to laugh your difficulties away.

Many people could not see that you were not merely throwing jokes around. You did not own life when you were alive. Now that you are alive in a different realm, you know for sure that you do not own life. You have watched God and Devil, gods and Ancestors, wondering whether *they* owned it, this thing called life. As far as you could see, nobody appeared to own it, judging by the way they too cast their eyes in the directions of our Hillbrow, Alexandra and Tiragalong, clicking their tongues with deep sadness or grim amusement when people devoured one another. You were right there with them, still on your way to finding out whether any of them owned life.

So, because you did not own life in this life, and because you do not own it now in the other life, you could not prevent Lerato from following your tracks. All you could do, child of our Tiragalong and Hillbrow, was to wait at the gates of Heaven. To wait for her so that you could give her a warm reception and celebrate your reunion. So that you could say to her:

Lerato, Bone of my Heart, welcome to our new Hillbrow . . .

*   *   *   *

You sat with Lerato for a long time at the gateway of Heaven, reminiscing about life in the University, in Parktown Village, in our Hillbrow and in Johannesburg generally. You took her through a linguistic trip of what had happened on the day you returned from our Tiragalong, with that strange loss of appetite for her food. She looked back at you with a protracted gaze and said:

Coward! You could have told me this long before today!

And then, out of her relief at discovering that she was not the only cause of your loss of zest for life, she began to tell you what it meant to live, or rather exist, with the memory of a loved one who had given you a vote of no confidence, which was what your suicide had demonstrated to her. It was that which influenced her own decision to exit this life by staging the same kind of drama that you had staged. Suicide; dying in a tablet-populated room in Alexandra, with no audience to watch, no dramatic fanfare, just the shock of her mother on arriving home from work to the gruesome discovery. She told you what it meant to exist with the fear that one's misdemeanour, one's open-thighedness – as people would construe her behaviour – would be uncovered; the anxiety at the prospect of facing an incredulous mother, whose heart would sink into the abyss of dismay on discovering, suddenly, that her much trusted daughter was, in effect, a murderess; of existing with her life clouded by constant brooding over what fellow University students would have to say about her sexual looseness, that had driven their beloved lecturer into the Dark Chamber of suicide; Terror haunting her consciousness and conscience with perpetual telephone calls that asserted his right to send his greedy, ever-erect penis to play between her supple thighs. All these thoughts and feelings, and more, she shared with you.

All of this, she said, while Sammy basked in the sanctuary of his insanity.

You both heaved a big sigh:

Poor Sammy!

Together, the two of you had then gone to meet your mother in the courtyard of Heaven. You introduced her to this former Johannesburger. Your mother had examined her looks carefully, the way old people in

Tiragalong are wont to do. You watched your mother's eyes contracting. They scrutinised Lerato from the feet, slowly moving up until they reached the level of her eyes. Your mother fixed a long stare there. And a gentle smile announced itself.

If we met in Tiragalong or in its neighbouring villages, I would have said that, indeed, men do spread like pumpkin plants. You look so much like Tshepo! I would not be surprised if I was told that something happened between his father and your mother.

She then began to tell the story of Tshepo's father and how he went to Johannesburg to look for work. And how the monstrous city swallowed him.

Those unknown dogs just plunged knives into this poor son of Tiragalong, she said. He died even before his son Tshepo could learn to recognise him, he was still such a baby.

Then, your mother took you and Lerato to the House of Heaven, where you met Tshepo and his father, Piet, who was Lerato's father too, but whom she had never known since he was killed before she was born. There too, was Tshepo's mother, who had died of grief when Tshepo was struck by lightning. She and Tshepo's father were finally reunited, although she did not yet know that her husband's heart was only partly here in Heaven, and partly in our Johannesburg, where Lerato's mother still was.

After your lengthy chat, it occurred to you that it was just about news time. So you went with Lerato to watch the TV in the Heaven lounge, while your mother continued her chat with fellow villagers or, as it now was, fellow Heaveners. After which Lerato suggested that you watch a movie together. You were not very keen on movies. When you were still living in our Parktown Village and Hillbrow, Lerato used to go to the cinema with Sammy while you did your academic work. But since she had just arrived in our Heaven, you decided that you would indulge her wish.

The movie for that evening was entitled *Times of our Lives*; a historical piece, you read in the weekly TV guide, that was based on the real life story of a man who had died just over two decades ago in Alexandra.

Welcome to our Alexandra . . . the movie began.

One morning (the story went), when Liz, Lerato's mother, was in the early stages of her pregnancy, Piet had kissed her goodbye in her servant's quarters' room in Honeydew, where the two were employed as gardener and domestic for a white couple. Piet was going to Alexandra, as he did every first Sunday of each month. The Tiragalong Burial Society, of which he was a member, gathered there to make their monthly contributions and to discuss whatever problems needed to be addressed. Piet ordinarily used these Sundays to visit those of his relatives and friends from Tiragalong who lived in Alexandra. One such relative was Molori. If cousins could be said to be close, then this was certainly the closest relationship.

Piet could not have known, on this particular Sunday, that Molori would not be happy to see him. Molori had just been home during the week, after receiving word that his mother had suddenly taken ill. Just like that. Found unconscious in her field by two boys who were grazing their small herd of bony cattle (drought ravaged the land at that time) close by. As boys often did, these two decided that they would enter one of the nearby fields to help themselves to melons. The hunger growls of their stomachs were growing fiercer than those of dogs looking for a fight. They had entered Molori's mother's field because it looked as if there was no one in there; nobody to begin preaching moral lessons to them, no one to lament the behaviour of the children of these days.

They stumbled across the mother. They would have tiptoed their way past had they thought that she was merely asleep. But they could see that was not the case. There were many ways of sleeping, some clearly better than others. But this way could not have been too good at all. Her head was resting on a small pile of mealies, and a hoe was still clasped loosely in her right hand. The left hand was lying just below her left breast, as if assuaging her heart. Her face was looking at the sky and the scorching sun was throwing its vicious rays into her unclosed, dazed eyes. The boys forgot their intentions. One ran to the nearest field in which he could see an adult, while the other just stood there, so scared of the smell of death hovering around him and Molori's mother that he regretted having thought of stealing a melon at all. When the nearest elder arrived, she shouted to So-and-so's mother to come and help her investigate what was going on. So the word went around in the fields of

Tiragalong – much faster than any radio news could have spread it – until all the fields were left empty. The first two women provided First Aid. By the time other adults arrived, Molori's mother was breathing somewhat better than before. A kindly man offered his wagon to transport her home. Although none knew for sure what the matter was, they all agreed that she must be taken to knowledgeable medicine people, immediately.

I hear there is a *Lepolantane* who has just visited Nnoko, the kindly man said. I am sure his medicines would be very good. They come from *Polantane* you see. Not from this village.

Polantane was a word of Sepedi coinage, a derivation of Blantyre, the capital of Malawi. And *Lepolantane* was a person from this place. Although *Mapolantane* had a reputation for being great bone throwers – though nobody appeared to know where this belief came from – references to *Mapolantane* were often negative. Initially, *Mapolantane* referred to the people from Blantyre; that was no longer the case. The word had been stretched and stretched like elastic. It now referred to any black non-South African who was from any African country. *Mapolantane* was a Tiragalong equivalent of *Makwerekwere*. And if children misbehaved, it was not unusual to hear an adult admonishing:

Now, you are not going to start behaving like a *Lepolantane*!

So Tiragalong felt that Molori's mother should be taken to this visitor who would probably shine his torch on her and tell her what or who was behind her sudden, strange illness that sent her oscillating between life and Heaven, torn between our world and that of the gods. Molori received a telephone message. He arrived on the same day.

He went to visit the suggested bone thrower. This bone thrower was one of the most famous – or notorious – in his region. He had a nose for witches that was truly impressive. He was the same bone thrower who had helped to sniff out the witch responsible for sending the lightning to strike Tshepo. It was only after the Comrades had burned her that it became apparent that they had burned the wrong person.

He was not one of those who said to you:

Put R20 down before I open the skin bag of bones. The bones cannot open their mouths to speak until they see what they are going to speak for.

No, he was not that type. His was a more subtle form of psychological blackmail. He told you what he had to tell you. Left you to thank him with whatever sum you thought his assistance deserved. Because his approach displayed a great deal of confidence in himself and his profession, as well as a sense of sympathy for his patients and other clients, he often ended up receiving higher rewards than he would have if he had fixed a fee. People were, in any case, afraid to offend such confident practitioners by insulting them with meagre rewards. Just in case they later bewitched them for such insults.

The bone thrower went with Molori to his village. At the bone thrower's suggestion, they waited until midnight before they left for Tiragalong, in order that others would not see from where Molori acquired his strengthening medicines.

When people know too much about you, it becomes easier for them to unseat you, the bone thrower had suggested. The problem is that they soon have an idea from where your medicines are dug, and what kinds of medicines you use. You see, it is easy to fight against what you know.

After giving Molori's mother a quick glance, even before taking out his bones, the bone thrower could see that it was good that they had rushed to call him. Or so he said. It was an extremely serious case. She could die at any time.

Given the urgency of the situation, the bone thrower immediately proceeded to the business of throwing the bones onto a grass mat that he carried with him. He looked hard at the bones, especially at the one that rolled away from the rest. He snorted and began to praise the bones, intimating in the process that his bones could tell nothing but the truth. And would the gods strike him dead if they told anything but the truth! And might the gods also strike him dead if he should interpret their narrative in any way but the correct one! He then began to speak fast, in a tongue Molori and his mother could not understand. Not that the mother could hear anything, anyway. Molori's uncle, who came to be the second ear – Molori being the first – also did not understand the utterances. After confusing his audience with the tongues in which he spoke, the bone thrower told them that he was chatting to his own Ancestors and the Ancestors of the house he was in. He was asking the Ancestors to bring their heads together and show his bones the truth about what could have led to the current illness of Molori's mother. And again he turned his attentive eye to the bone that had rolled away from the rest.

It says that those who get waylaid by their own blood can have no feet with which to run away from the dangerous fire, he began.

He went on and on, talking in proverbs and riddles and metaphors, until he finally got to the point in plain language.

You see, this woman here has been bewitched by her own blood. To the east of this homestead, there is a close relative whose heart is burning with jealousy. Who does not like the fact that her son is working as a gardener for a white family, while your mother's son works in an office. She actually wanted to bewitch *you* (looking at Molori) but the Ancestors said No. They protected you from her strong medicines. But the medicines had to work, you see. So they vented their rage on your mother.

He then went on to describe the physical looks of the close relative in question. Molori and his uncle nodded with every detail. At times Molori gasped with disbelief.

The bone thrower had not come by his impressive reputation for nothing. He was a clever man. He knew the importance of knowing people. Everywhere he stayed, he would make it his business to get to know the community, the clan links, the family histories and other such useful details. Very little happened that escaped his eyes and ears.

After the bone thrower had left, having strengthened both mother and son against the jealous malice of their enemies, Molori and his uncle looked at each other in silence for a very long while. It was unbelievable the things that relatives could do to each other. The bone thrower's descriptions, they agreed, pointed squarely to Piet's mother and to Piet himself. According to the bone thrower, it was Piet's constant jealous complaining about the success of Molori that had spurred his mother to act as she absorbed the bitterness and ill will of her son.

It did not occur to Molori and his uncle to doubt the bone thrower's insights. His accurate knowedge of their family affairs was too impressive; where else could such knowledge have come from, they reasoned, other than from his reading of the bones? The uncle also reminded Molori about the Tiragalong saying: witches have no distinct skin colour through which other people can recognise and identify them. Piet and his mother might put on the act of being good people. They might pretend honest affection for their relatives. But who was to say that that was not the art of witches? The true insides of a person are hidden in the dark corners of their chests and breasts, where our naked eyes cannot penetrate.

On the night following their strengthening, Molori could hardly sleep. Every time sleep encroached upon him he would see, in his dreams, a huge snake squeezing itself into his room through a tiny space between the door and the floor. The space was so tiny that no snake of any size, let alone such a big one, could ever hope to go through. Yet this one managed. Molori would wake with a start each time, just before it poured its venom into his heels through its bright fangs. He would imagine that the snake was Piet. Or Piet's mother. Or both, merged into one, the way things are possible in Dreamland; coming to do their evil purpose, and failing. He discovered for himself that this strengthening did help. Every time he woke up, he was angrier – and more frightened of his cousin . . .

When Molori left for his shack in Alexandra, the uncle having reassured him that he would see to the well-being of Molori's mother, and to the administration of medicines and other things, he was full of purpose. Piet, of course, on his visit to Molori's house that Sunday, could have had no idea what was going through Molori's mind. It was their first meeting since those-who-had-eyes had seen through mother and son's ill will and revealed their hidden lairs of witchcraft. Piet had no way of knowing that in Molori's eyes he had become a practitioner of the art of prowling in the night. How could he have known? He who did not even know how to mix herbs for his ordinary cold. He would not have been aware that he was now the enemy of his beloved cousin and his whole family. Nor could he have guessed that his cousin had organised with two men, professional killers that he had been introduced to by a fellow worker, to do what everyone knew was worth doing with night prowlers – especially when their skills turned you or your loved ones into their prey.

A short time later, Piet was found lying dead on the pavement of an Alexandra street, next to the men's hostel where it was suspected that the knifers stayed . . .

As you, Refentše, watched the tragedy of this life story unfolding, as you sat in the lounge of Heaven and pondered the complex paradox of life, death and everything in between, you seemed to see, simultaneously, the vibrating panorama of Hillbrow and all its multitudinous life stories, conducting themselves in the milk, honey and bile regions of your own expanding brain. Your head became incredibly painful. You heard the echoes of *Welcome to our Hillbrow* . . . hitting relentlessly against your skull, as if trying to fight their way out of the bony encasement. Your skull threatened to collapse at any moment, causing you the worst headache known to humanity. Your head spun at untold speed and you became intensely dizzy in these hot, whirling webs of sensory input, your memory picking out choice words here, scenes there . . . the infinite fragments combining and recombining in the containing frame of your head. Until the roaring pressure of your skull finally exploded:

Welcome to our Hillbrow . . . Welcome to our Alexandra . . . Welcome to our Tiragalong in Johannesburg . . .

Refilwe

efilwe would not have known the story of Piet's
death. Nor that he was in love with Liz, Lerato's
mother, mainly because their love relationship
was cut short before Piet could blunder, could let out
the secret affair for people of Tiragalong to pass along,
with their ever-wagging tongues, to his wife in the
village. All Refilwe knew was that Lerato was a
Johannesburger. But that did not stop her from
speculating the rest. What she decided to share with
Tiragalong were her suspicions that Lerato was not just
a Johannesburger, in the way that people born in the
city could be said to be Johannesburgers. She was far
worse than these; she had the blood of *Makwerekwere*

running in her veins. Her mother was one of these women who could not say no to any drop of semen found flowing aimlessly in the streets. So she had courted a stranger's sperm, as it flew its way round the streets of our Hillbrow.

Refilwe was not a woman of vulgar words. The daughters and sons of Tiragalong were the ones who rephrased her story in such terms. By the time her version gained momentum, there was no one to contradict it. Lerato had already followed the Bone of her Heart into the Dark Chamber. Your body and hers were buried under six feet of our country.

It was true to say, Refentše, that Refilwe loved you deeply. When she learnt that you had staged your drama from the twentieth floor of your building, her heart broke and bled. The blood mixed with the sorrowful floods of tears that gushed out her eyes. It was a cruel loss for her, the loss of the future Bone of her Heart. She had not given up on the idea that one day you would be tired of these Johannesburg women, that your thoughts would then turn back to your home girl. She knew, like all Tiragalong, that there was always a return to the ruins; only to the womb was there no return. Also, Tiragalong had a saying that those who had smelled at each other's bottoms never really separated. So Refilwe always had hope. Until, that is, you crushed it with your emotional adventurousness, letting your heart plunge into a pool of love with a Johannesburger. Your suicide crushed Refilwe's hope for good, and the blood and tears of sorrow that gushed from the pieces almost drowned her heart.

It was true, of course, that Lerato's heart also drowned in such floods of sorrow. If Lerato's heart could be said to be more grieved than Refilwe's, it was only because the former saw her assisting role in the drama all too clearly. Refilwe's grief was without that crippling sense of guilt. She had done nothing to assist your death. Had she not tried, in fact, to save you from your raging emotional storms of infatuation with the Johannesburg woman? The fragments of the story that Sammy had, earlier, come to circulate in Tiragalong made a lot of sense to her. What else did you, Refentše, child of Tiragalong and Hillbrow, expect from such a woman? Refilwe also wondered about Sammy's moral behaviour. Running after your love with similar blindness. But Sammy was peripheral to her concerns. Her sore heart came back again and again to you and what she termed your emotional naïveté; to your revealing conduct towards her on the day that you had visited her for a home-made, nourishing meal in her bachelor flat at Vickers Place.

You had arrived on time at Refilwe's flat. You were generally a very punctual person. You had left the office early on that day, because you wanted to see Lerato before you went to Refilwe's. You wanted to drink from what Stimela called *Fountains of Love* – quench your emotional thirst, so that other honeyed waters would not seduce you. You needed the strengthening that Lerato's kisses were capable of providing to your all-too-human heart. So you were confident that you were strong when Refilwe opened the door of her flat to you; even so, at the back of your mind was the nagging thought that you were very human. Your impulsive act with Bohlale was stored in your memory, reminding you of what, just like Refilwe, you were capable of. At that stage, you never imagined that Sammy and Lerato, too, were human enough to do as you had done.

Refilwe knew how to treat her guests. She started you off with music of your choice. She knew you had always loved Stimela's music. The song she put on, *See the World through the Eyes of a Child . . .* was released in 1994, by which time you and she had long since ceased to be the Bones of each other's Hearts. But it was a good choice all the same, since it had always been a favourite of yours.

Stimela's song was not attractive to you simply because it was nice music. You loved it – and in fact the whole album – because of the associations the words had for you. *See the World through the Eyes of a Child . . .* in particular, was special to you because it was a song about a neglected, homeless child, exposed to much street violence and blood, and subsequently grown to be scared of darkness. It was a song of prolonged pain and suffering; but it was also a song of hope and love. It reminded you strongly of your own loneliness and fear of rejection at certain dark times of your life.

Refilwe could not know the significance the song had for you. She did not know that Stimela's music was part of the shared history between you and Lerato. Her welcome was intended to please you. With music. With food. With words. With flesh. With everything in her flat that could recall for you the pleasure of her company and contribute towards returning you to the memorable days of bliss that you had shared together.

As the good-smelling vegetable soup simmered on the stove, she took out her archives of photographs. You knew some of them well. The ones of you and her entwined in each other's embraces, your glowing faces proclaiming that none of the outrageous storms of life would ever send the strong walls of your love castle tumbling down. Then there were other photos that she had taken with the lover that, as she explained, came after you – after your hot head had decided that her betraying lapses meant that she did not love you. A pity you had to find out about them, because she had by then resolved to sever the ties with those worthless boys; men, in her opinion, only because their *things* were protected from the gaze of the public by pairs of trousers, and because they had whiskers that they mistook for beards. She severed the ties on the same day that you left her, Refentše, child of Tiragalong and Hillbrow and Heaven. She almost hated you for that desertion. But she also realised that you did not understand; that she was just a youngster learning the ways of life, searching for the green pastures that we all searched for in life, that you, too, in your own way, were also searching for.

The lover whose photo you were looking at now was a stranger to you. The relationship, she told you, only lasted two months because she found him, one fine day, kissing another woman. It was not just a kiss of cousins or friends greeting each other. It was a kiss of tongues locked into each other, salivating and swallowing the juices of the mouths. It was a kiss whose strength was reinforced by hands fondling each other's breasts and chest, moving down their bodies to provide the same measures of attention and care to the southern hemispheres. There were sweet moans that took her mind back, bitterly, to the recent days when those moans would be exchanged between herself and the lover. Like you, she admitted, she could forgive without forgetting. Which is why she dumped him immediately. The way you did with her.

The two of you enjoyed your supper together. You talked about many things. You talked about education. She told you that she intended to enrol for a higher degree part-time with the University of the Witwatersrand. You said, what a good idea! You knew that she was capable of doing well in whatever she chose. Even of going to read for her Masters degree in Oxford, never mind Wits, if that's what she wanted. That was the night you first planted the idea of Oxford in her mind, urging her to consider it, to dare to dream big, and not confine her ambitions to the smaller pastures of home.

It was only after the meal, with Stimela's *Fountains of Love* playing again, providing the musical background to your togetherness, that Refilwe suddenly looked up and said:

Oh, that is a beautiful song.

You agreed. And then she said:

See the World through the Eyes of a Child . . . Have

you ever thought about the words? Really thought about them?

You said: Indeed I have . . .

She looked at you with the gentle, but concentrated, look she was capable of giving. She sighed, almost seeming to suppress the sigh. There was a long silence in which she divided her visual attention between you and the space in the flat. Although you were not sure what to expect, you could see that it was going to be heavy, whatever would follow. You could see that her heart was full. With what? You were unsure, child of Tiragalong and Hillbrow. You imagined that someone might have disappointed her recently. A new lover perhaps? Not likely. She had just told you that she was single. When a tiny drop of tears betrayed her, you could not help moving closer to her. You embraced her, without voicing any words. You waited for her to be able to speak, to volunteer whatever it was she was going to say. In your warm embrace that she loved so much, she again sighed a forlorn sigh and said:

I love you Refentše. I wish we could go back to those days of yesteryear. When we were still children trying to find our way through the valleys and hills of life. When we could still live without cynicism. When we still had the innocence of children . . .

She choked. Her heart was too full to hold her tears any longer. They gushed out. You, too, were moved. You remembered the days she was referring to. You remembered the disappointment that followed those days. The beauty and the bitterness of love. You remembered learning by pure chance about her four other ongoing relationships, simply because one of the lovers boasted about this to you, when he gave you a lift one night from Pietersburg to Tiragalong.

Refilwe's words also reminded you of the first love you had. It was not a relationship in the usual sense. You simply loved the woman, who loved you back, but who was honest enough to tell you that although she loved you, she was not prepared to have a relationship with you because you did not own a car. That day, the fact of your family's poverty had stared you cruelly in the face like a mesmerising snake.

You had asked yourself painfully about the value of love and life, if both could not bring fulfilment to a hopeful heart. Your natural tendency to brooding had thrown you into deep melancholy. You had had your first thoughts about committing suicide then. It was Sammy who set you straight. When, after months of silent suffering, you confided your misery to him, Sammy had advised that life was still full of vast possibility, even without the woman. He talked at length about how your education would ensure in the future that you could provide not just for your own life, but for your mother's and your future family's – when, not if, you had one. He went on to mention, with his usual generous patience, the list of people from neighbouring villages who had managed to free themselves from the shackles of poverty through hard work and education. You had the capacity for hard work. And, as all in Tiragalong knew, you were already well on your way to achieving the best in education. He had talked about many women of re-markable worth, in Tiragalong and its neighbourhood, who loved you as much as you loved the greedy woman; who did not make cars a pre-condition for family life.

No! Sammy had said, one does not contemplate something as final as suicide when one's future is so bright.

Sammy was not a careless friend who would go around singing about the miseries confided to him. He never told anyone about your time of crisis. The secret remained between the two of you.

Now, Refilwe reminded you of all the sweetness and bitterness of your past love and life. It was then that you thought of Lerato. And you knew that you could not betray her. As much as you still loved Refilwe – for sep-aration is in itself never an end of love – you knew that you were not, this time at least, going to betray the Bone of your Heart.

So you kept the embrace in check. You reminded Refilwe that you had a relationship that you could not simply break off without a reason to do so. Yes, you knew she loved you, just as you loved her once, and continued to do even after your disappointment in her. But she must realise that love did not always result in a love relationship. She could still rely on you for sup-port. As a friend. You held no grudges against her for the past. You genuinely wished her well in life, with everything, including the love life that, you hoped, she would be able to build. You would be there for her if ever she needed your help. But not as a lover, not so long as you were still in love with Lerato.

But, Refilwe argued, since you have admitted that you love us both, would you not feel more at home in the arms of a child of Tiragalong? We know what Jo'burg women can do to a man . . . !

You said: Yes, some Jo'burg women are certainly terrible. But the same can be said of some Tiragalong women. Are some of them not known for throwing love potions into the food and drink of their husbands or illicit lovers? Love potions that are sometimes so strong that they turned the men into madmen?

You knew, as you said this, that you did not really believe in such things. But you also knew that Refilwe could not easily dismiss your words; nobody from Tiragalong could afford to treat such stories with the scepticism that you thought they deserved. Too many people in the village had been victims of these accusations. So it was quite legitimate to cite these ex-amples. It was also convenient, because Refilwe, who oscillated between believing in witchcraft and not believing in it, had never quite learnt to dismiss it entirely. For the purposes of your argument, it was a weakness you could capitalise on.

When you left Refilwe, you were aware that she was an unhappy woman. Although she had betrayed you in the past, you could believe that she still loved you now – a love that, in some ways, you returned. You also knew that she was disappointed that a child of Tiragalong like you should find vulgar Johannesburgers equal to – or better partners than – the women of the village.

Nonetheless, you trusted her thinking capacity. You

imagined she would think through these difficult issues. That later, when she had a good partner of her own, she would come back to you and report that life was great. The two of you had continued to keep in touch. And since nothing obvious appeared to be bothering her, you assumed – wrongly, as events were to show – that her understanding of the situation had dawned earlier than anticipated.

Refilwe on the Move

Tiragalong was quite impressed when it heard that Refilwe was going to do her Masters degree overseas. Impressed, without knowing that she would shock them on her return. That was just over two years after Refentše's suicide.

She found herself unable to proceed with her Masters immediately, in the year following Refentše's death, as she would have liked to do. This was because her old father had passed away in the same year, which meant that she had to become the sole pap-winner for her family. Although it was not a very poor family, the death of the father suddenly rendered it so. Her two elder sisters were already married. But her younger sister and brother still needed to complete their school and University studies. Her mother was simply not in a position to see them through this financially arduous task. And then, Refilwe also had to take care of the mother herself.

So Refilwe remained for two more years with the publishing house that had given her her first job. When her immediate superior resigned, Refilwe was promoted to the position of Commissioning Editor. She was excited by the challenge of the new position and looked forward to earning a better salary. But she soon discovered the frustrations that went with her new and prestigious position. Although she knew what good books looked like, the company kept on reminding her that good books were only those that could get a school prescription. What frustrated her so much was the extent to which publishing was in many ways out of touch with the language and events of everyday life.

It was a very different story with other creative forms; music for instance. In the music trade, unlike in publishing, producers and public alike were receptive to work that broke new ground. To songs that spoke in the hard language that people used in their everyday lives. That was why rap and kwaito sold so well, including the more vulgar forms of both genres, that kept the tongues of elders clicking with disgust at the immorality of the children of these days. It was that same receptivity that explained why a television drama like *Yizo Yizo*, which portrayed tsotsi school children ever proving to be a menace to their teachers and fellow pupils, was so popular. Or notorious. Looked at either way, *Yizo Yizo* managed to secure a wide reception because people's taste for the popular and notorious had always been enthusiastic. People enjoyed works which shocked them. Which made them think and reminded them that life was not a long night of cosiness. Works which were not simply pleasing arrangements of text or tune, but which commented on the hard realities of life, drawn from and finding support in personal and social experiences.

A school kid shot ten fellow pupils and then himself in Los Angeles . . . In Soweto, a gun-toting youngster shot his school principal dead and fled in the principal's new car . . . In Alexandra, five school children held the whole staff hostage during a lunch-time break . . . The police were still investigating in all these cases . . .

So a fairly open-minded Commissioning Editor in Sepedi had to be frustrated when she could not take a crop of newly-emerging, critical writers onto her list; writers who, while they appreciated the value of linguistic euphemism, also had their bright eyes open to its moral and philosophical dangers.

It was because of these frustrations, because she had come to value so greatly the importance of literary honesty and risk-taking, that Refilwe appreciated Refentše's short story so much; his story that looked at AIDS and *Makwerekwere* and the many-sidedness of life and love in our Hillbrow and Tiragalong and everywhere. His scarecrow heroine was a big influence on Refilwe's thinking. She had read the story many times, and each time it made her weep anew. Partly because of the memories it brought of Refentše. And partly because it made her see herself and her own prejudices in a different light. Since his death, she had had much cause to rethink her own stereotypes of Johannesburg women.

Because, despite her broken-heartedness over Refentše's suicide, despite her bitter spreading of stories about Lerato in her grief and jealousy, Refilwe had gradually come to share Refentše's opinion that the people of Tiragalong were, in fact, no better or worse than Johannesburgers. She came to see that Hillbrowans were not merely the tiny section of the population who were born and grew up in our Hillbrow, but people from all over the country, and other countries – people like herself, in fact – who entered our Hillbrow with all sorts of good and evil intentions.

It was for all these reasons – the memories she needed to leave behind, her dissatisfaction over her job, her restless need to explore new territory, and Refentše's frequently expressed opinion that she should not sell her talents short – that she decided to apply to do her Masters in Oxford rather than at Wits.

When she told her mother of her determination to apply to Oxford Brookes University, the news was not welcomed. Her mother was quick to remind her of the need for her to be the financial support of the family.

Besides, daughter, she said, how can you leave me in a state of such poor health? Who will take care of me? Yes, you can send me money, but do you think I love money more than I love you? Oh what is wrong with the children of today?

When at last the gods mercifully released her mother from the sharp claws of her illness, Refilwe decided, once and for all, that this time nothing was going to hold her back. She lost no time in submitting her application. And, before long, was informed that she had been offered a place on the MA programme in Publishing and Media Studies.

Oxford, Seat of Learning (as your publicity proclaims), here comes a daughter of Tiragalong and – despite her occasional protests to the contrary – of Hillbrow. She is thirsty for knowledge and the other promised fruits which a scary flight across thousands and thousands of kilometres of land and ocean, at twelve kilometres above sea level, will bring in reach.

Refilwe, child of Tiragalong and Hillbrow, welcome to our England . . .

Although she was coming to England for the first time, Refilwe was not an absolute stranger to the country. Which is to say that she knew at least one soul there who could welcome her and show her around the place. She had first met Jackie when the latter came to do voluntary work, after her first degree, in South Africa. Jackie was one of those people from moneyed families who could afford to spend a year doing useful but unpaid work. She came to teach at Tiragalong High in 1996, the same year that Refilwe had started her Assistant Editor's job in Johannesburg. Refilwe had gone back home over one of the long weekends to see her family. While there, she had visited her old school to say hello to the principal and some of her teacher friends.

That was how she and Jackie first met. They took to each other from the first and subsequently, when Jackie visited Johannesburg – which she did a number of times that year – she would stay at Refilwe's Vickers Place flat.

When Jackie left for Oxford, they had continued to communicate, postally, telephonically and via e-mail. They exchanged birthday and other presents, especially books that they both regarded as good reads: winners of the Booker Prize, the CNA Literary Prize, the M-Net Book Prize, the Noma Award for Publishing in Africa, the Commonwealth Writer's Prize and others. They exchanged jokes and problems, sharing thoughts on pressing matters of love and life. Except that love matters were often a one-sided affair, because there were none that had materialised in Refilwe's life. Sure, there were people she met who interested her. They told her how clean their hearts were in her much-prized presence; how her mere existence whitened their hearts much better than any brand of OMO washing powder could ever hope to do. Their tongues rolled out words of sweetness that no honey could surpass. Their words tickled her, washed over her heart and left no lasting trace. She never overcame her disappointment over matters of love. She loved Refentše too strongly to let go even when he had passed away.

The September of the adventurous year of 1998 finally arrived. Refilwe found Jackie waiting for her at Heathrow International Airport, where the latter treated her friend to a traditional English breakfast of bacon and eggs. Such traditional English food was so common in South Africa that Refilwe enjoyed it not because of any English novelty, but because its taste blended with the joy of reunion. She found less enjoyment in the English beer, when she was introduced to it. Traditional English ale was not refrigerated. Like many South Africans, Refilwe could hardly imagine how anyone could swallow an unrefrigerated beer in the name of tradition. At home, when men were desperate for a drink and the only sacred waters flowing in the streams of their vicinity were hot ones, they might force themselves to take a glass or two, while the rest was rushed into the deep-freeze for quick cooling action. Refilwe's imagination, trying to draw a comparison between this ale and the tastes of all things she knew, concluded that it tasted like nothing so much as hot urine. She had once tasted cow urine in Tiragalong. As children, they were taught that cattle urine, drunk as soon as it poured into the ground from the backsides of the animals, was good for people learning how to whistle loudly. Refilwe had taken the required step in that direction – and nearly vomited. She had spat it out the instant that the liquid hit her tongue. But the taste lingered unforgettably in her memory, unpleasantly recalled by the taste of this ale. Fortunately, global imperatives had encouraged the South African Breweries to bring to our Heathrow their own ale brand – the famous *taste that stood the test of time.* Refilwe gladly switched her loyalty to that.

After their breakfast, the reunited friends caught the Oxford Tube bus straight to the Seat of Learning. They arrived, almost at midday, at Oxford Brookes

University, alighting at the corner of Gipsy Lane and Headington Road, where our University was. Jackie thought that it would be a good idea to go straight to the administration block and get all the formalities of enrolment over and done with. Papers were produced and signed. No, Refilwe did not have to register with the Oxford police, as many Africans, including South Africans during the Apartheid days, had to do. South Africans, black and white, were very fine people these days, thanks to the release of Rolihlahla Mandela from Robben Island in 1990 and his push for the 1994 demo- cratic elections. Was that not a miracle! No violence – at least not on any large scale – as had been anticipated by cynics. South African Broadcasting Corporation, Brit- ish Broadcasting Corporation, Cable News Network and other news media set themselves up for the coverage of the massive political violence that was not to be. Was that not an indication of the civilising power of old man Mandela? These and other such laudatory noises ap- peared forgetful of the fact that Mandela was not the only player in this game of politics. In any event, Refilwe did not have to sign with the Oxford police.

She was of course grateful, but not entirely happy about her privileged South African status. Even before she arrived in our Oxford, she could not enjoy the bad treatment that she had witnessed the Nigerians and Algerians, for example, receiving at the hands of the Customs officials at our Heathrow. She was reminded by these scenes of Alan Hill's book, *In Pursuit of Publishing*, in which he records the humiliation he suffered on arriving at Jan Smuts Airport – now Johannesburg International Airport – in the murky days of Apartheid rule. When, as a British citizen, he was attended to last by Customs officials because his bags had to be thoroughly searched. He records the shock he felt at such treatment, because when he was in Nigeria and Ghana prior to that, he had been treated like an angel by the authorities. Such scenes repeat themselves frequently in our England in the new millennium, in the early part of the twenty-first century. Nigerians and Algerians are treated like pariahs in our white civilisation. Refilwe learnt that the supposed reason for the treatment was that they were all drug dealers, or arms smugglers, engaged in trading weapons for their civil war-wracked countries. They were criminals masquerading as students, or as professionals coming into our England to negotiate reputable business deals. Heathrow was full of Nigerians and Algerians with their luggage turned inside out. It was not the responsibility of the Customs officials to return the insides of the bags to their former neat condition. Nor to offer apologies to those – a significant number of them – found to be innocent as far as the carrying of drugs and ammunitions was concerned. There were also significant numbers of Africans who were being put through lengthy medical checks. Whereas South Africans just walked through the rituals quickly, filling in a form or two to say:

Yes I saw a doctor before I left, and no, I am definitely not HIV-friendly . . .

It was not the same for these other Africans. These

Africans from the West were the sole bringers of AIDS and all sorts of other dirty illnesses to this centre of human civilisation. Their passports were scrutinised, signatures checked, double checked and triple checked. Our Heathrow strongly reminded Refilwe of our Hillbrow and the xenophobia it engendered. She learnt there, at our Heathrow, that there was another word for foreigners that was not very different in connotation from *Makwerekwere* or *Mapolantane*. Except that it was a much more widely used term: *Africans*.

Refilwe was to observe, in Oxford, that people there talked about Africans and South Africans. These Oxfordians who talked so distinctly about Africa and South Africa were themselves a hybrid of native Oxfordians and those who had acquired the citizenship by other means. All those we called by the term Oxfordian, without distinguishing whether they were, indeed, born Oxfordians, or English, or something else. It was no different to the way we generalised about Hillbrowans without venturing to clarify what we meant. Refilwe remembered the time a South African film director was beaten up. He was almost ushered into the World of the Gods because he was mistaken for a *Lekwerekwere*. She was reminded of this every time she heard Oxfordians talking about Africans and South Africans. She learnt that to come from South Africa and to come from Africa were not the same thing at all in the estimation of numerous Oxfordians. She also learnt that when people talked about South Africa, they meant Johannesburg, Cape Town and Durban. They had also heard of Soweto, the biggest black township in South Africa, about ten kilometres to the south-west of Johannesburg. For them, the cities were all white, while Soweto was black. Black in human skin colour, but also black in morals.

When Refilwe once said to a fellow student at *Morals*, the student pub at Morrell Hall Residence, that there was a place in Johannesburg, full of grime and crime, called Hillbrow (she suppressed the beautiful side of it for impact), the student was shocked. He could not believe it. Whites could surely not be guilty of indulging in criminal activities to the extent that Refilwe said they did? Refilwe remained adamant that, yes, there were white prostitutes in our Hillbrow. And white criminals who sold drugs, who were happy to see *Makwerekwere* serving as the butt of the vicious criticism and hostility from those who insisted that *they* were the only legitimate children of the country. There were whites who sold liquor and glue to street children. Who owned those shops in that Hillbrow? Mostly whites. And the bottle stores? Well, no doubt there were many black supervisors . . . but the ownership was largely white. Refilwe said:

That is your Johannesburg for you . . . !

And Cape Town? her listeners enquired. Refilwe had not been to the Mother City, as some South Africans called it (because that was where the first whites from the sea had landed). She knew it was a beautiful place, if photographs were anything to go by. She also knew that gangsters featured significantly in the news there in the late 1990s. Robbers had attacked a police station, walking out with a large cache of guns. Gangsters and rival gangsters regularly fought it out in public places, trying to prove who the real owners of our Cape Town were. These were just a few examples of the kind of shocking things that went on right there in the Mother City of beautiful landscapes and cool breezes.

Hillbrow in Hillbrow. Hillbrow in Cape Town. Cape Town in Hillbrow. Oxford in both. Both in Oxford. Welcome to our All . . .

On her arrival at Oxford Brookes University, Refilwe was offered student accommodation at Morrell Hall in Marston, five minutes' walk from the Headington Hill Campus of the University, where the Publishing and Media Studies building was located. If you drove there from the corner of Gipsy Lane and Headington Road you would take the route to the city centre, drive past the main entrance to the Headington Hill Campus, and turn right into Marston Road. You might decide to stop there, at the corner of Marston and Headington, to enjoy a drink at the Irish pub. From the pub the first street (not the pathway) to your right would be John Garne Way, which made a T-junction with Marston Road. You would drive up the gentle slope of John Garne Way to Morrell Hall, where it came to an end as a cul-de-sac.

After sorting herself out with the administration there, Refilwe was shown to Block J. The section of Block J that she would stay in was J9. It comprised five bed-sitting rooms with a shared bathroom, toilet, lounge and kitchen. She was dismayed when she walked into her room for the first time and realised how tiny the windows were. She discovered too, that they did not open widely enough for her liking. For the first few days that she spent in that room, she suffered claustrophobia. She would wake up at awkward times of the night with a feeling that someone had put a plastic bag across her mouth and over her nose so that she could not breathe. It was better before sleep time. At least then she could sit in the lounge and read, or chat with her four J9 mates.

None of the five was a native of Oxford, nor of any part of England. They were South African, Indian, Irish, Spanish and Greek – a United Nations of sorts. Which was why it was easy for them to start a conversation at their first meeting. All anyone needed to say was:

Ah! These English are really strange! They simply greet you and from then on, they pretend that you no longer exist!

Yes, it's called minding one's own business, I'm told, another might comment.

They're as cold as their weather, someone else would contribute.

The topic of the English would then be discussed at length. Refilwe once acknowledged that she liked their professionalism and their sense of dedication to their duties. She had innocently made the observation one day in *Morals*; upon which, an angry fellow student had shouted:

Yes – professional even in their racism!

She only learnt afterwards that the student had failed his first assignment and attributed his low marks to the fact that he was the only African in a class of white Europeans and Americans.

The J9 group lived well together. They often shared food, washed dishes together, and spent at least an hour, nearly every evening, just chatting, catching up with the events of the day, exchanging music likes and dislikes, talking about their assignments. And making plans to invite friends over for a special meal that they called Chicken J9, because the way the chicken was prepared was unusual to all of them. It was a United Nations menu – composite of cooking methods from different countries. Jackie introduced them to what became their favourite hang-out, a pub called *Jude the Obscure* in Walton Street, near the city centre, close to the great Oxford University Press. It was important, one might have said, to have knowledge and relaxation so close to each other, since hunger for knowledge and thirst for relaxation were twin desires, one complementing the other.

The inhabitants of J9 liked the idea of visiting *Jude the Obscure* – and it was not really out of any love for Thomas Hardy's novel. They were attracted there be-cause, Jackie told them, every Wednesday evening from eight until the pubs closed just after eleven, there were live poetry readings, as well as readings of all kinds of fiction. There would also be live music – pop, rock & roll, jazz and other sorts. *Jude the Obscure* was undoubtedly the place to be on Wednesday evenings if you were in Oxford. Especially if, like Refilwe and the other inhabitants of J9, you knew that there was as much knowledge and relaxation to be found in pubs as there was in books.

And so one typically cold evening – all the evenings were decidedly cold and damp in November – they accompanied Jackie to *Jude the Obscure*. Refilwe was very favourably struck by the place, as were her fellow J9 inhabitants. There were many fellow students, as she discovered after a while, mixing easily and happily with non-students, many people who discussed books while simultaneously indulging in beer. Guinness ruled the evenings. Posters and cartoons of James Joyce, Oscar Wilde, George Bernard Shaw, Seamus Deane and others lined the walls. There were quotable quotes from *The Importance of Being Ernest*, *A Portrait of the Artist as a Young Man*, *Reading in the Dark*, *Arms and the Man* and other great works. The owner of the pub was a well-read Irishman; well-read at least in Irish literature. He was able to engage in complex discussions on Irish literature and nationalism and was willing to listen and be informed on literatures from other parts of the world. He bought Zakes Mda's *Ways of Dying* after Refilwe had recommended it very strongly, with the enthusiasm of a South African who thought that her country had not been left behind when it came to quality literary output. Here was a strange story – both funny and sad – about Toloki, a man who hoped to found the profession of mourning. To professionalise the art of mourning at funerals, in the same way that there are medical and other professions. Toloki was an ordinary person, with truly individual mourning skills, in the process of inventing an extraordinary profession. As she recommended it, Refilwe could not have known that her family would soon have cause to mourn on her own behalf. Theirs would not be professional mourning, but it would be sincere. Had she known, then, that she would have a new occasion for brooding in this Oxford of ours, she might have wondered whether she would have the strength of Noria, the Bone of Toloki's Heart, to deal with the tremendous burden of the notorious disease that was to make her the talk of our Tiragalong and Hillbrow and so many other places. Here was Refilwe herself, bringing our *Ways of Dying*, ways of mourning, and ways of wondering to our *Jude the Obscure*.

Refilwe was later to tell Jackie and the fellow J9 inhabitants that *Jude the Obscure* reminded her of *Sweeney's*, a pub in the Braamfontein Centre, just opposite the University of the Witwatersrand. The mood was very comparable, although *Sweeney's* did not have the poetry readings and other performances. It was simply a pub where Witsies – as the students of the University of the Witwatersrand were fondly and sometimes derogatorily called – and other people came on Friday evenings to celebrate their small victories, to drown the sorrows of the dying week and to anticipate and strengthen themselves for those of the following week. There, *the taste that stood the test of time* was a constant sight on their tables and in their hands as they laughed, talked or danced the evening away. *Jude the*

Obscure reminded Refilwe of *Sweeney's* before it closed down, for reasons unknown to her, at the end of the year in which Refentše decided to stage his drama in our Hillbrow.

Refilwe remembered the day she met Refentše at *Sweeney's* during their reunion, before Lerato came to collect him on her way back to Hillbrow. She did not reveal to her friends the huge waves of raging nostalgia that *Jude the Obscure* caused to surface in her heart as she remembered that day. She did not tell them of the host of happy and unhappy memories that *Jude the Obscure* invoked of her beloved Refentše, his spectacular departure and her unrequited love. Nor could they know that all this time, while outwardly appearing to enjoy herself – smiling and laughing too much for her inward brooding to show – Refilwe's attention was closely fixed on somebody across the way; a young man of about her own age, who from the distance looked so much like Refentše (except that his complexion was a shade darker), that she could have sworn that he had come back to our world.

Refilwe did not go to sleep until very late that night. How could she fall asleep, when her mind was full of the sight of Refentše – her Refentše, miraculously transported here to our *Jude the Obscure* (as it seemed to her), with no Lerato to compete for his attention? Every time her eyelids dropped, heavy with exhaustion, she would snap them open again, as if hoping to witness some confirmation that the man she saw in her dreams was indeed Refentše. The stranger-who-was-not-a-stranger teased her quite often that night. He came carrying *the taste that stood the test of time* in his hands, despite the fact that one hardly ever saw any South African brew in our *Jude the Obscure*. He visited her in dreams that substituted Vickers Place for Morrell Hall.

In the early hours of the morning, as deep sleep finally defeated her, the inevitable happened. She was rolling her tongue around Refentše's, with her soft hands brushing his chest gently. He held her tightly, not wanting to lose her. They kissed with mouths and tongues as well as with the southern hemispheres of their bodies. Refilwe was sweating hard when she jumped out of the dream. Her bedding was so wet one would have thought it had been caught in torrents of rain.

She sighed a regretful sigh; a sigh of remembrance for our Hillbrow, for the good old days of our Tiragalong, before chance and a broken-down minibus taxi led Refentše to the terrible discovery of her other four love relationships. That was the day she discovered that forgiveness and continuation of relationship was not necessarily one and the same thing. She could not get out of her mind the stranger with Refentše's beloved face, turning his steady, welcoming gaze in her direction in our *Jude the Obscure*. And she recalled with longing the sensations of joy and brooding that the gaze had summoned in her heart.

The following Wednesday seemed far too long in coming. When it did arrive, the stranger-whose-face-was-Refentše's was there again, as she had hoped, turning the same compelling gaze her way. She decided to risk closer contact. There would be nothing wrong with initiating a chat with a fellow student (of life, even if not of the University) in this Oxford pub in which resided so many of the memory landscapes of home. She did come closer. She dared to start a conversation. She complicated her life.

Refentše, looking down from Heaven, helpless to intervene, could not help wishing as he watched that he was God, or the gods, and owned this world of ours. That he had the power to persuade Tiragalong and its judgemental children to suspend their judgement, to try and understand that Refilwe was only doing what we all did; searching for happiness, for meaning in life. Holding on to fragile straws here, to strong branches there. Stumbling and getting up again to continue the crazy journey across the Macbeth stage of life, where we are only the actors in search of the right cues.

But of course Refentše was neither God nor gods. He was not even sure that any of them would look with kindness on Refilwe's quest for a fulfilling life. He only knew, as he watched her from his high vantage point, that God and the gods of our happiness were more likely to be found in Hillbrow and Oxford and Tiragalong – everywhere and anywhere except in the Heaven that we read about in the Big Book. God, gods and the Devil – that horned, black monster holding his large fork in his hideous hands – lived in the skulls and hearts of the people taking their unplanned and haphazard journeys through our world. Refentše knew only too well that Refilwe was going to bear the brunt of their wrath when she went back to our Tiragalong. These gods and devils of our Tiragalong would say:

So, you thought the ones in Johannesburg were not bad enough! You had to import a worse example for yourself!

They would say this, because the stranger-with-Refentše's-face that Refilwe met in our *Jude the Obscure* was a Nigerian in search of green pastures in our Oxford. He and Refilwe did find some green pastures in each other's embraces that following Wednesday evening. They had Refentše's blessings. His only wish was that he owned life, so that he could force those on Earth to give the lovers their blessings too.

Refentše's love, Lerato, noticed that something was eating at him. She asked the Bone of her Heart what the matter was. He said:

It's nothing – just a movie I've been watching on TV. It's a sad story about a man and his woman who have fallen prey to AIDS. They are sharing the fatal infection with each other. When they go back to their respective villages and the people there learn that they are suffering from AIDS, they say:

Indeed! Is it not known what the fruit of sin is?

Refilwe had come to our *Jude the Obscure* and loved it, despite the sorrow it woke in her. She loved it the way she loved Hillbrow and Tiragalong, the way she loved life. If Refentše were still alive, he might have written a poem for her, called *For Refilwe Who is No More …* It would have been her eulogy.

Because soon, very soon, she would be joining

Refentše, Lerato, Bohlale, Tshepo and the others in the World of our Heaven. Together, they would talk about Hillbrow and Tiragalong and Oxford. They would share their thoughts about love, AIDS and xenophobia. They would discuss ways of turning their spoken and unspoken thoughts into written fictions and poems.

And as Refilwe comes to this part of her journey to AIDS and Tiragalong condemning her and the Bone of her Heart and Refilwe herself reaping the bitter fruits of the xenophobic prejudice that she had helped to sow Hillbrow and Tiragalong flowing into each other in her consciousness with her new understanding of life love and prejudice gained in our Oxford and Heathrow Oxford London and Lagos demystified Tiragalong sweating its way through the scary invasion of AIDS apparently aggressively sown by migrants and all witch-craft becoming less colourful and glamorous in the face of this killer disease the impact of which could be seen with the naked human eye without the assistance of diviners and bone throwers love crossing oceans and flying over highest mountains life reconsidered in the light of harsh possibilities of rural virtues laid bare under the eyes of human microscopes all these and many more things flowing into and blending with Refilwe's expanding consciousness . . .

Welcome to the World of our Humanity . . .

The Returnee

Refilwe returned home in September of 1999, a year after her departure from our Hillbrow and Tiragalong. She returned, as they say, with a degree in her bag. Troubled by her rapid deterioration. Swearing to herself that she would soon join her beloved Refentše in Heaven to await the coming of the other Bone of her Heart. As soon as her Nigerian had learnt about his illness, he had bid Refilwe goodbye in order to go and waste away at home, in Nigeria. He would have loved to come back with Refilwe to our Hillbrow and Tiragalong. But he did not want to become someone else's burden. Refilwe, for her part, was torn between going with him to Nigeria and returning to our

Hillbrow and Tiragalong. She wanted to die here at home, to be buried in the sun-scorched lands of the Northern Province that was filled with dry grass and tree leaves turned white, like bleached bones. She wanted to be laid to rest in our Tiragalong, even if it meant exiting this world amidst the ignorant talk of people who turned diseases into crimes. She knew, as Lerato had known, that it was difficult for a woman to face her friends, colleagues and the whole community, and say her name, when they all judged her to be just a loose pair of thighs with voracious appetite – thighs in search of wandering penises to come and caress them. Now it was her turn to be the accused. She now was the one over whom the gods and devils of Tiragalong would sit in judgement. But Refilwe had also learnt in her difficulties to look at life from many sides. It was not just Tiragalong and Hillbrow, but our Nigerian brother . . . Refentše . . . her J9 friends . . . and many other people who formed part of her consciousness.

These other voices within her consciousness told her that there were those who loved her still. For them, she would try to live as long as she could. She did not want them to have to suffer the pain that she had suffered, of wondering what they could have done, or not done, said or not said, to keep her from exiting this life prematurely. She thought deeply about Refentše at this time. She thought of him doing his spectacular jump from the twentieth floor in Van der Merwe street, after he had chosen his *Lekwerekwere* woman over her. She understood now that there were many ways of dying, that the choice between suicide and life was not merely a choice between stupidity and intelligence, that sometimes, when people threw their own life away, it was because they were intelligent and courageous enough to see and admit that they did not own this life.

She thought of her own vow that she would soon join her Refentše and the other Bone of her Heart in Heaven. But it would not be through suicide. Her mind was not ready to give up the fight. She thought of the Dark Chamber, beckoning to her seductively from six feet under the Earth. And she said:

No, I am not going in there yet . . .

But she also knew in her heart that she was finished already. When she and her Nigerian were told that they had AIDS, they were also given to know that they had both been HIV-positive for a long time. Refilwe, in particular, must have been infected for a decade or so. Except that she had not known that. So when the disease struck, it seemed that it came suddenly, with no warning. It came with the speed of lightning and was just as fatal. The cold, damp weather of Oxford, as well as her brooding concern about her loved ones at home, did not make her life any easier. Her brooding was as bad as the encroaching English autumn weather; just as bad as all the ailments that did the rounds in her body. With such a concoction of ailments, bad weather and brooding, Refilwe knew she had to be finished quickly.

When she arrived at Johannesburg International Airport, where her family and friends had gathered to welcome her, she wondered whether she could brave the keen grief in their eyes. Against their will, they failed to disguise the fact that they had already given her up to the gods. Her thinness made their attempts at disguise impossible. Her younger brother began to sob as soon as his eyes landed on her bony frame. Her hair was as thin and fine as the fur of a kitten, her eyes almost popping out their sockets. She looked so fragile you would have thought that her clothes were too heavy for her. Refilwe's brave heart had been eaten away by thoughts of home and Heaven; by her worry over what they would say when she finally arrived and also over the other Bone of her Heart, wasting away alone in far-away Nigeria. She missed him, but she was also glad that he wasn't with her, having to face the Tiragalong prejudice, knowing they would want to pin the blame for her disease on his head. She remembered Refentše telling her how the superintendent of his building hated *Makwerekwere*:

It used to be fine in Hillbrow, until the Nigerians came.

Now she herself was, by association, one of the hated *Makwerekwere*. Convenient scapegoat for everything that goes wrong in people's lives. She had learnt a lot in Oxford, more than the degree in her bag implied. The Refilwe who returned was a very different person from the one who had left.

Refilwe's brother's sobs pricked the hearts of those that came to meet her. They knew the moment they saw her, that the African Potato, a medicinal plant that looked like the bulb of a beetroot, would not be able to cure her. The African Potato was said by some to work much better than Virodene (which was then the latest pharmaceutical invention for the treatment of AIDS) providing the disease was caught in the initial stages. It was also rumoured to be far more powerful than Viagra, for men whose performance in bed was less than sparkling. The African Potato was said to out-perform all other pharmaceutical inventions. But Refilwe's family knew just by looking at her that she was beyond this or any other help. She was at an advanced stage in her journey through this world.

They had already known before they saw her that she was dying, because she had written a letter to her family to let them know that she had AIDS. She had also told them the story of her relationship with our Nigerian brother, and that he too had AIDS. All of this they knew. But knowledge arriving through fast-mail was not vivid enough to bring the point home. Now it hit with the force of the fatal lightning that struck Tshepo, as they encountered her physical presence at the Johannesburg International Airport.

Refilwe, you were very grieved by this show. You felt sorry for those who loved you so much and expressed it so openly. You knew it was not intentional that they should depress you. They spoke no words to express their muddy whirlpools of feeling. But as you walked into the parking lot, where your younger brother had parked your car, which he had been taking care of in your absence, you heard a voice whispering:

But she is so thin! Look at how the clothes are

simply hanging on her bony shoulders. And look at those sticks of legs!

The voice was sensitive to your feelings, whispering in order that you would not hear. Articulating, you knew, the collective thoughts of your family and friends. You paid attention to those words. They were words that you knew you would hear often, if you lived long enough. You knew, too, that living long enough was absolutely guaranteed, because every moment now was long enough. If such words did not actually come from people's mouths, then they simply rang inside your own head. You had turned into the scarecrow woman of Refentše's fiction. Now, having met your family and friends, you began to wonder why you had not rather passed away in our Oxford, to return as a corpse flying over the Atlantic Ocean, twelve kilometres above sea level, nine hundred and forty kilometres per hour. You wondered why you had not passed away in that centre of civilisation, because you were beginning to discover that grief, incarnated in the gloomy faces of your family and friends, could be just as fatal as lightning and AIDS.

Refilwe, child of our land and other lands, welcome back to our Hillbrow . . .

You will be in Tiragalong in a day or two, as you wish to see the place before disease and grief sink you further towards the Dark Chamber. You will be there and the old men and women of the village will be saying:

Welcome back Refilwe . . .

And behind your back:

Are those clothes hanging on her bones not making her look just like a scarecrow . . . ?

The young ones, too, will welcome you to our Tiragalong. Some might speak their minds straight into your face; like your male peers whose former sexual advances you had rejected in very strong words. They would say:

But what is the use of sanctity if it does not shield you from AIDS?

They were going to see AIDS incarnated. They did not realise that several of the people they had buried in the past two years were victims of AIDS. It was easy to be ignorant of this, because this disease lent itself to lies. Such people were thought to have died of flu, or of stomach-ache. Bone throwers sniffed out the witches responsible, and they were subsequently necklaced.

Stories of Refilwe's decline brewed along the village grapevines, spilling out into the streets of Tiragalong and then to other areas; via the N1 . . . Telkom . . . Vodacom . . . MTN. Refilwe the Incarnation of AIDS . . . Former beauty turned into a scarecrow . . . An example of what Oxford, Johannesburg and *Makwerekwere* could do to the careless thighs of the otherwise virtuous ones of Tiragalong.

Refilwe, welcome to our Tiragalong, where your fellow villagers are awaiting your arrival. They are expecting soon to sing *We are just Passers-by on this Earth*. Before long, they will be coining words and phrases about your departure to other Worlds. Maybe they have already begun to do so. Perhaps they are even now saying about your impending death:

Oh Refilwe! She left us, yes, these two days past. Departed for Nigeria!

Or:

Aren't the birds becoming a problem in the fields now? Where is that scarecrow . . . ?

Linguistic chisels, furthering the process of carving your death that AIDS had begun. Speeding the process up. As if, the sooner you died, the better for their belief in the evil of *Makwerekwere* and the AIDS they are said to bring.

You know what treatment to anticipate. You think back to the days of milk and honey that you spent with our Nigerian brother, who is the embodiment of Refentše, the first Bone of your Heart. You remember when it all started; Refentše, watching you through the Nigerian's eyes in *Jude the Obscure*, on that fateful night when the past came to roost in the present. In your heart, the two are one. Tiragalong and Nigeria, blended without distinction.

Now you can sigh with resignation, child of our Hillbrow and Tiragalong and Oxford, as you think of your imminent entry into Heaven. You are wondering what Refentše will say to you when he sees you again. You know that you are not the same Refilwe that you were when he was alive. You can no longer hide behind your bias against *Makwerekwere*. You do not blame them for the troubles in your life, as you once did. You have come to understand that you too are a Hillbrowan. An Alexandran. A Johannesburger. An Oxfordian. A *Lekwerekwere*, just like those you once held in such contempt. The semen and blood of *Makwerekwere* flows in your Tiragalong and Hillbrow veins. Now you are the talk of the town and the village, and there is no Refentše to add his voice to the few voices of reason who say that disease is just disease. That choice is choice, and no one in particular can be blamed for the spread of AIDS. That Tiragalong should know well enough that its children are no better than others; the necklacing of witches . . . cousins stabbing and shooting each other in Alexandra and Hillbrow . . . Terror raping innocent and defenceless women and girls in our Hillbrow – all these things are enough evidence of that.

But Refentše is not here to come to your defence. And you, Refilwe, are now one more sad example of the dangers of love gone wild. Tiragalong will in future admonish its children by saying:

Now, you – do not behave like Refilwe, or you will come to the same end!

In the meantime you were treated to Chicken Hillbrow by your loving family and friends. You were treated to Chicken Tiragalong. You learnt that someone was planning to buy the space that was *Sweeney's*, retain the name, and begin to operate it as it used to be before. Life was going on, as it would continue to go on, long after you had bid this world farewell. Soon, you would arrive in Heaven, where you would meet Refentše, Lerato and the others. You would chat with them about the continuation of life. You would share with each other your understanding of what the reality of Heaven is; that what makes it accessible, is that it exists in the imagination of those who commemorate our worldly life. Who, through the stories that they tell of us, continue to celebrate or condemn our existence even after we have passed on from this Earth.

Heaven is the world of our continuing existence, located in the memory and consciousness of those who live with us and after us. It is the archive that those we left behind keep visiting and revisiting; digging this out, suppressing or burying that. Continually reconfiguring the stories of our lives, as if they alone hold the real and true version. Just as you, Refilwe, tried to reconfigure the story of Refentše; just as Tiragalong now is going to do the same with you. Heaven can also be Hell, depending on the nature of our continuing existence in the memories and consciousness of the living.

Like Refentše, the first real Bone of your Heart, you too have had your fair taste of the sweet and bitter juices of life, that ooze through the bones of our Tiragalong and Alexandra, Hillbrow and Oxford.

Refilwe, Child of our World and other Worlds . . .

Welcome to our Heaven . . .